TRIPLOIDY

TRIPLOIDY

THE ARCHON SEQUENCE

BILL DESMEDT

WFP
WordFire Press

Ebook ISBN: 978-1-68057-290-2
Trade Paperback ISBN: 978-1-68057-289-6

Cover design by Janet McDonald
Cover artwork images by Adobe Stock

Kevin J. Anderson, Art Director
Published by
WordFire Press, LLC
PO Box 1840
Monument CO 80132
Kevin J. Anderson & Rebecca Moesta, Publishers
WordFire Press Ebook Edition 2022
WordFire Press Trade Paperback Edition 2022
WordFire Press Hardcover Edition 2022
Printed in the USA
Join our WordFire Press Readers Group for
sneak previews, updates, new projects, and giveaways.
Sign up at wordfirepress.com

CONTENTS

DEDICATION

For Kaylie
August 13, 1986
Precious Child, Beautiful Star,
This one's for you.

PROLOGUE
SHOUTING IN THE JUNGLE

May 24, 1999

...all the talk about alien invasion and
the danger of messaging extraterrestrial intelligence
I regard as idle and pseudoscientific.

—Aleksandr Leonidovich Zaitsev

Once upon a time, in a place not so very far, far away, there lived a man who was convinced he knew better than the whole of the human race what was good for it.

That wasn't the problem. There have always been such men, at all times and in all places.

No, the problem was, at this particular once-upon-a-time-and-place, this particular man was in a position to act on that conviction.

His name was Aleksandr Leonidovich Zaitsev, and his position was that of head of the Yevpatoria RT-70 Planetary Radar in Crimea—a facility which boasted a parabolic dish antenna some seventy meters in diameter and ranked at the time of our telling as the third largest radio telescope in the world. More to the point, Yevpatoria was also the only installation of its size equipped to both receive signals from outer space and to send them as well.

And it was this that Zaitsev intended to do. On the evening of May 24th in the penultimate year of the second millennium, he pointed the Yevpatoria dish toward the heavens and transmitted the first of several so-called "Cosmic Call" messages.

Whatever their extraliterary historical significance, these messages were hardly paragons of style or substance: Basically a binary "Rosetta Stone" composed by Stephane Dumas and Yvan Dutil which proceeded from rudimentary arithmetic to higher order math and physics, supplemented with a smorgasbord of text, audio, and video from ordinary citizens around the world. If there was one worrisome feature of Dumas and Dutil's contribution to Cosmic Call, it was that their "primer" included a representation of the nucleotides making up deoxyribonucleic acid, better known by its initialism: DNA.

Still, in the end it wasn't the message's form or content that mattered. Rather, it was the simple fact that, for the three hour and fifty-five minute duration of the transmission, the Yevpatoria signal increased the radio visibility of the Earth by *four* orders of magnitude. Briefly, in its limited frequency band and along its narrow line of sight, the Earth shone ten thousand times brighter than the sun.

It was, then, not without a certain cosmic irony that Zaitsev's surname derived from "*zayats*"—the Russian word for "rabbit." Because he was indeed like some foolish little rabbit hopping down a dark and dangerous bunny trail, shouting at the top of his lungs and blithely advertising his presence to whatever predators might be lurking in the surrounding jungle.

And not just his own presence—all of Earth's as well.

Zaitsev's target on that lovely, late-spring evening was the yellow dwarf star 16 Cygni B, one hub of a triple-star system seventy light-years away in the northwest corner of that patch of sky named for the constellation Cygnus the Swan. Or more precisely, not the star itself, but rather its companion world. For three years prior, in 1996, 16 Cygni B had become one of the first stars to be confirmed as hosting an extrasolar planet. True, 16 Cygni Bb, as the exoplanet was designated, was a super-Jupiter. It weighed in at 2.4 Jovian masses and as such was an unpromising abode for the proverbial life as we know it. Still, where there was one planet, might there not be other, smaller, more hospitable worlds, as yet undetected, circling that same distant sun?

In any case, we wouldn't have long—on cosmic timescales, at least—to wait before finding out: Zaitsev's signal was scheduled to traverse the seventy light-years from Earth to 16 Cygni Bb and arrive there in November of 2069. Allow, say, a year for the putative inhabitants to mull a response, then another seven decades for the lightspeed return trip to Earth, and we might hope to receive a reply around the year 2140.

It was the possible form such a reply might take that rendered Zaitsev's project deeply problematic, at least in some quarters. Even the doyens of the old Search for Extraterrestrial Intelligence (SETI) enterprise expressed reservations when contemplating the downside risk of this new *Active*-SETI endeavor—this initiative to dispense with decades of passive listening in favor of actually *doing* something.

Those downside risks were not inconsiderable. The Cosmic Call critics protested that we shouldn't call attention to ourselves when for all we knew our transmissions might be received by some real-world equivalents of H.G. Wells's "intellects vast and cool and unsympathetic." These beings might—out of paranoia or sheer malevolence—reply with relativistic impactors or cosmic computer viruses or interstellar laser beams that would set our sky aflame?

Zaitsev would have none of it. Dismissing the hand-wringing of the naysayers as "idle and pseudoscientific," he vowed to carry on. And, given he had access to the requisite technology, how could anyone realistically hope to stop him?

In point of fact, Zaitsev was right: None of his detractors' nightmare scenarios would come to pass.

What *would* come to pass instead was much, much swifter and much, much worse.

For in another, unimaginably further-removed time and place, a wise and ancient race had—after eons of godlike accomplishment—collectively resolved to depart the plane of material existence for their own unfathomable reasons.

But not before leaving behind, in their terrible benevolence, a parting gift.

That gift takes the form of a spherical wavefront, a globe of coherent light. Expanding ever outward from a point of origin long since lost in time and space, it is now moving through one of the spiral arms of the Milky Way galaxy.

It is a wavefront with a difference, overlaid with cunningly crafted interference patterns that split a portion of its beams off from the prime vector and bend them back in a "delay line." Of such elemental circuitry is fashioned the functional equivalents of XORs, NAND gates, and the rest of the low-level instructional menagerie that make up the firmware of a standard computer.

Save that this computer's "ware" is decidedly *not* "firm." Rather, it is a gossamer, its components forged of trimeric light. That is, light endowed with an infinitesimal smidgen of mass. Hence it is capable of interacting with itself by binding triplets of its constituent photons into the bosonic equivalent of molecules.

Save also that, inspirited by architectures of superhuman subtlety, all those simple intangible piece-parts are capable of self-assembling into something no mere earthbound computer can hope to match—a photonic intelligence.

An intelligence tasked with a single purpose: to bestow the blessings of its creators' beneficence on any and all inhabited planets within its ever-expanding ken.

Admittedly, it is not *much* of an intelligence. Smeared out across the surface area of a sphere already some tens of thousands of light-years in radius and growing all the time, that which propagates outward in all directions from its long-lost source is by now a mere shadow of its original self. Merely a photonic entity that, after a seeming eternity of attenuating dilation, boasts all the smarts of your average amoeba.

It is, in fact, just smart enough to detect, at any given point on its enormous capture surface, one of a small number of trigger events.

The least significant of such triggers is the sort of transmission represented by the Cosmic Call, still only twelve years along on its seven-decade journey to 16 Cygni Bb at the moment when it intersects the wavefront entity. In and of itself, Zaitsev's four-hour message burst might seem too transitory, too weak, and too primitive content-wise to warrant attention. But interstellar space is vast, and life-bearing bodies are few and far between. Even the least promising candidate for Transfiguration deserves, at a minimum, *some* consideration.

The entity marginally alters its incorporeal internal dynamics to bestow that minimum: Rippling outward from the point of intersection, the wavefront ceases to expand and begins to fold back in on itself. Refractive structures coalesce to focus light and logic on the bare-bones intellect which had first encountered the message from Earth. It's a shift that augments the entity's processing power, and with that power, its perspicacity, until at last the nascent photonic entity achieves a modicum of mindfulness.

And waits to see what would happen next.

What would happen next was once upon *this* time.

PART 1

ARRIVAL

MORNING, LAST DAY OF AUTUMN

0700 HOURS: INTO THE LIGHT

"Jon, I'm pregnant."

Whatever effect Marianna Bonaventure might have anticipated this announcement having, it had not included the little convertible being braked hard enough to trigger the automatic seatbelt locks.

One moment, she and Jonathan Knox had been cruising up the stretch of El Camino Real that ran through the wilds of Big Sur, California. The next, they were sitting on the shoulder, engine ticking, clouds of road dust rising around them.

Jon was staring at her intently from the driver's seat, silently studying her face.

Marianna's heart sank. *Oh, God. He thinks I'm trying to trap him!*

"No worries." She affected a nonchalance she didn't really feel. "I'll be fine—"

Jon leaned over and kissed her on the lips.

"No," he said. "*We'll* be fine."

Marianna Knox née Bonaventure smiled at the memory, then winced.

Soon now. Her night-long labor was entering its final throes as the first rays of dawn spilled across the birthing bed. Jon stood beside her in the delivery room, holding her hand. She could tell by his abstracted look that he was trying to recall the finer points of his Lamaze training. Typical male: he was having enough trouble remembering to breathe himself, much less urge her to do so.

To Marianna, the intervals between contractions felt like floating becalmed in the gentle swells of a tranquil sea. Then without warning a storm surge of agony would hoist her up, up into the sky, rip through her, and tumble her over and over. It crested and, as quickly as it had come, it was gone. Then she was sliding down the long, liquid slope into the trough, gasping for breath and bracing for the next wave.

Her uterus pulsed like a metronome—a metronome whose rhythm was accelerating, beats coming faster and faster—nature's countdown.

But in between the beats came moments of introspection, thoughts about what it all meant. According to all the mother-to-be self-helps she'd read, she was about to embark upon the "adventure of a lifetime."

Well, maybe so. But considering all the adventures in Marianna's lifetime to date, there would be some stiff competition for that accolade.

She smiled again, then frowned, recalling a summer evening she and Jon had spent together two years back, cruising the North Atlantic onboard a corporate megayacht as big as a city block. All while, in the depths below them, a secret installation ensconced in the summit of an undersea mountain ticked down the final hours till Armageddon.

The memory whirled away into darkness as another contraction crashed into her, this one feeling for all the world as if a giant's hand gripped her innards and squeezed them, trying to push them down, down, and out of her body cavity altogether.

Then it passed, leaving her drifting among reminiscences once again.

Reminiscences of a night in a futuristically palatial compound overlooking the Pacific, the scene of a technology launch gone horribly, earth-shatteringly awry, threatening to merge all the world's intellects into a single, mindless meta-consciousness, and of a last-second intervention from an unexpected quarter.

Reminiscences segueing into that long walk up the aisle on the arm of her boss, Euripides "Pete" Aristos who stood in for her late father. She walked toward a beaming Jon, accompanied by his unlikely best man, Finley "Mycroft" Laurence, who seemed determined to make up for the groom's evident lack of nervousness with a double helping of his usual agoraphobia.

And then the contractions were upon her again.

In the two and a half years they'd been together, Jonathan Knox had watched while Marianna poleaxed a hulking Gruzian hitman, had gazed through someone else's eyes as she consigned an Iranian terrorist to a hell of his own devising, preventing gigadeaths in the process. Both times.

But this—this was far and away the bravest thing he had ever seen her do.

Yet, as proud as he was of his partner—his new wife, the soon-to-be mother of their child—Knox also felt ... helpless, useless, superfluous. Not for the first time, he wondered what in the hell he was supposed to be doing here. Providing back rubs and foot massages? Timing contractions? Helping allay anxieties?

As far as that last part was concerned, he might as well forget about it. If anything, Knox was more anxious even than Marianna herself.

"Jon?" Marianna's whisper intruded upon his self-indulgent funk. "Could I have a sip of water, please?"

Knox inserted a straw in the water bottle and brought it to her lips. Holding the bottle in position with one hand, he sponged Marianna's forehead with the other.

"You're doing fine, *solnyshka.*" He used the Russian word for "sunshine," the term of endearment not only evoking the brightening dawn, but also serving as a reminder of the assignment that had first brought them together. "Just a little bit longer now."

"Just a little bit longer now" would also have been the thought entertained by the insubstantial instrumentalities currently traversing near-Earth space. Had they been capable of thought.

As matters stood, all that these rudimentary ripples of trimeric light could manage was to receive a feed from the Washington Square relay station and retransmit it to the wavefront's central processing locus out past the orbit of Saturn. That feed, in turn, contained, suitably amplified, the feeble emanations from the monitors in the delivery room at Saint Bartholomew where Marianna Knox lay giving birth.

The photonic entity that was called "the Emissary" by its human servants received that feed. Only then it could fully formulate the thought:

"Just a little bit longer now, and the Transfiguration can begin."

With a final, shuddering convulsion, Marianna delivered. It was a little girl, whom she and Jon had agreed to name Persephone. Exhausted as she was, Marianna had to smile: it had taken some persuading to get Jon on board with the mythological reference.

"Persephone?" had been his initial response when she'd broached it to him.

"Mom and Dad would've loved it." They would have, too. Marianna's deceased parents were both students of Greek antiquity. "Why? What's wrong with Persephone?"

"It's just that—well, what are the other kids going to call her?"

"That's the whole point: Persephone is nickname proof. I never liked nicknames."

But Jon was thinking out loud now. "Persey. Persey Knox. Has kind of a ring to it."

Marianna found herself wishing her mother could be here to see this, to see what she and Jon had made. Because Persephone was perfect.

"Nine pounds, two ounces," the assistant was calling out. "Twenty-one and a half inches long."

Going to be a tall *girl!* The right number of fingers and toes, and ...

What had gone wrong with the light? The early morning sunbeams now streaming down through the skylight seemed ... *off* somehow. Dimming, though there wasn't a cloud in the sky. Then brightening again, but now with a bluish tinge, which quickly cycled through all the colors of the rainbow, looking like light filtered through stained glass. And, caught in the sunbeams, bathed in the unearthly radiance, Persephone nestled peacefully in a nurse's arms.

Too peacefully. *Why isn't she crying?*

And why was the doctor monitoring the DNA microarray looking so worried all of a sudden?

0800 HOURS: CONSULT

"Oh, I wasn't expecting anything like this." Marianna took in the tasteful decor of the postpartum suite as the nurse eased her off the gurney and onto a split-king adjustable bed. "It's all just so—so welcoming."

Not to mention upscale. A kitchenette was tucked into a nook to one side of the room, while an entertainment center with flatscreen TV graced the far corner. A picture window set in the exterior wall gave a view of Central Park, snow-dusted fields and bare-limbed trees aglow in early morning light.

"And look, Jon." She patted the other side of the mattress. "There's room for you to sleep here with us too. We can spend Persephone's first night together as a family. How did you ever arrange all this?"

"That's just it," he said, sitting down beside her on the bed and looking around at the library stocked with bestsellers and first-run DVDs. "I didn't. I mean, I booked us a private room, but I had no idea it would come with all these, um, inclusions."

He turned to where the nurse was just opening the door to leave. "How about it, nurse—is this what we ordered?"

The young woman flushed. "No sir, your reservation was

upgraded to this neonatal palliative care unit. It's just Saint Bartholomew's way, in situations like this, of trying to make our patients as comfortable as possible."

"What would really make me comfortable," Marianna told her, "would be for me to see my baby. I barely got a chance to hold her before they took her away. For tests, they said. Can you tell us what's going on?"

The nurse wasn't meeting Marianna's gaze. "The doctor will be by to see you soon. He'll explain everything," she said hastily. Then she slipped out the door and was gone.

Marianna turned to her husband, reached out to grip his hand. "'Situations like this.' What do you think she meant by that, Jon? What situation?"

Suddenly, the suite, which had felt so bright and cheery a moment ago, seemed to darken and close in on her. Marianna was having trouble breathing.

Is something wrong with my baby?

Jon took her into his arms, held her tight. "It's nothing. I'm sure it's nothing," he soothed, though his tone belied his words.

There was a knock at the door. Another nurse came in, this one older, more businesslike, sporting carefully coifed gray hair and armed with a clipboard.

And questions.

Disquieting questions they were, too. Like: "Have you ever been exposed to high levels of radiation?"

Well, she had, of course. She and Jon both, in a place called Antipode Station, set into an undersea mountaintop at the crest of the mid-Atlantic rift. On the other hand, telling the nurse that would be about six kinds of security violation.

Instead, Marianna asked, "What's all this about? Why can't I see my daughter?"

"You can. Of course you can. It's just that there's something the doctor will have to discuss with you first. Both of you."

Marianna had been expecting their obstetrician, but when a doctor finally did put in an appearance, it was a stranger. A tubby, balding, ginger-bearded stranger who introduced himself as Malcolm Burke, board certified in neonatal genetics.

Doctor Burke took a seat in the palliative suite's commodious armchair and crossed his ample legs. He tried and failed to look Marianna in the eye. "Uh, I'm afraid I've got some bad news about your daughter. The results of her postnatal gene sequencing are in, and they demonstrate conclusively that..." He paused, as if struggling to recall the child's name. "... that, uh, Persephone is suffering from a disorder known as triploidy."

Those last words tumbled out in a rush.

"I'm sorry, doctor," Marianna said. "I don't know what that means."

The doctor sighed. "Where do I begin? You know our genetic material—the DNA, uh, call it a blueprint, if you will, that makes us who and what we are? Well, it comes in the form of tiny structures called chromosomes? And that we humans are diploid organisms, meaning that all of those chromosomes consist of two strands of DNA?"

Marianna nodded, trying to rein in her mounting anxiety.

"Well, then." Burke waved a pudgy hand. "Those DNA strands are called chromatids. And since, in the human body, the nucleus of every cell contains twenty-three chromosomes, that makes for twenty-three pairs of chromatids, or forty-six in all. With the exception of the human egg and sperm cells, that is—they each have only half that number. That's how sexual reproduction works, actually. When the two gametes— that is, the mother's egg cell and the father's sperm cell— come together, they each contribute one half of the chromatids needed to form the chromosomes for a new individual, a new baby inheriting half its characteristics from each parent."

Doctor Burke paused. "Sorry, that's a bit off-topic," he said, before beginning again. "So twenty-three pairs of chromatids—of DNA strands, that is—in each cell ..."

He blinked, swallowed. "Unless," he went on, "something goes wrong."

The bottom dropped out of Marianna's stomach. She gripped Jon's arm with hands gone suddenly cold.

Jon found his voice first. "What are you telling us, doctor? What *is* triploidy?"

The doctor looked away. "A rare condition. At least it's rare to see it in a child come to full term like this."

"Because it usually goes away before then?" Something in Jon's tone told Marianna that he didn't believe that was it.

"No, Mr. Knox." Burke shook his head sadly. "Because the pregnancy almost always ends in a spontaneous miscarriage long before the child can be born."

"But, but—why?"

"Remember how I was saying that, reproductive cells aside, there are twenty-three pairs of those DNA strands in the nucleus of every cell in a human body? Well, that's in a normal human body. In your daughter's case—and, God help me, I don't know how we could have missed this till now—" The doctor swallowed again. "Persephone has an entire extra set of strands. Not twenty-three pairs, but twenty-three, uh, triples, if you will—sixty-nine chromatids in all, instead of the normal forty-six."

"And that's bad, because ...?"

"Because adding a third strand of DNA to even just a single one of those twenty-three chromosomes—a condition known as trisomy—is a recipe for genetic disaster. When that happens to chromosome twenty-one, for instance, it results in Down syndrome. And here we're talking about *all twenty-three* chromosomes. Triploidy isn't just bad, Mr. Knox. It's a death sentence."

Jon lurched as if someone had punched him in the gut.

Into the silence that followed, her eyes brimming with sudden tears, Marianna said, "You're telling us our baby has—has died?"

"No, not yet, Ms. Knox, but I'm afraid it's inevitable. There's no way to sugarcoat this: triploidy is, simply speaking, incompatible with life. The mortality rate is one hundred percent, without exception. The longest surviving triploid baby on record lived only ten and a half months and seemed to be in constant pain all that time."

"Persephone is—is suffering?"

"No, strangely enough, other than running a slight fever, she seems to be resting comfortably. And that's not the only strange thing ..."

"What else?" Jon asked tonelessly.

"Well, simply the fact that we were only able to establish this diagnosis postpartum. Nowadays, routine prenatal genetic screening should have detected the syndrome early in the first trimester. Not to mention that there should have been physical abnormalities in the fetus, observable via ultrasound by about the twelfth week of pregnancy—though those abnormalities vary with the specific type of triploidy."

Doctor Burke must've read the incomprehension in their eyes, because he elaborated: "Digynic triploidy is where the extra DNA strands are contributed by the mother; it presents as an abnormally small fetal body size, among other symptoms. The diandric variant, where the extra chromatids come from the father, isn't as obvious. But it can be more dangerous to the mother, since it can induce preeclampsia and elevate blood pressure to life-threatening levels. In either case, given there's zero chance of the infant surviving, the recommendation would have been to abort as soon as the condition was confirmed."

"But none of that happened."

"No, what's different here is that, up until the moment of her birth, Persephone's test results, including the prepartum gene sequencing we conducted shortly after Ms. Knox was admitted, all seemed perfectly normal. But triploidy—any garden-variety triploidy, that is—is present from the moment of conception. There's no known mechanism by which it could be induced postpartum, after the child is born, that is. And yet that seems to be what's happening here. Quite frankly, we're at a loss. Both to that, and—"

"There's something else?"

Marianna knew that tone: Jon was getting exasperated.

"Well, it's just that triploidy is usually a global syndrome, affecting all the cells of the body. Which only makes sense when you consider that it's present in the fertilized egg from the outset and propagates with every cell division of the embryo from there on."

"And that's not the case here?"

Burke shook his head. "There *is* a less severe variant called mosaic triploidy, where only some of the body's cells are affected. But what we're seeing isn't consistent with that diagnosis either."

"What *are* you seeing?"

"As far as we can tell, Persephone's condition seems to have started out localized, like a mosaic. Confined to the central nervous system, in fact—which would be fatal in and of itself. But unlike a stable mosaic, and again—for reasons we don't understand—it's spreading throughout the rest of her body's cells. Quite frankly, we don't know what to make of it. The disorder is progressing in a manner that we've never observed before."

"Can't you arrest that progress somehow?" Jon asked.

"Not without knowing what's causing it. I'm sorry, Mr.

Knox, but our best guess at this point is, once the effect has run its course, the outcome will be the same."

"Our daughter is going to die, you're saying?"

Burke shrank into himself, gave a miserable shrug. "If it's any consolation ..."

"Yes?"

"Well, as I said, triploidy is rare, almost vanishingly so. There's no reason the two of you couldn't have another baby. A healthy one."

Marianna, tears streaming down her face now, said, "No, I want *this* baby."

For his part, Knox stood there stunned. Over the past nine months he'd had ample opportunity to ponder what kind of a father he'd be—and kept coming up with answers he didn't like. Truth be told, he was pretty sure he'd suck at it.

Face it, Knox, he'd told himself any number of times. *You live in your head too much to shoulder the responsibilities of parenthood.*

Though, over the past couple of years of their relationship, Marianna had gone some distance toward engaging him with the world outside his own thoughts. More properly, engaging with her and, through her, the world. Unsettling though it had been at times—especially the occasional brushes with death that Marianna's day job seemed to entail—he'd found himself unexpectedly liking it. Enough so that he even found himself getting used to married life.

Still, becoming a father was a whole different level of commitment—one he'd doubted he'd ever be ready to take on.

All things considered, he ought to be feeling relief of a sort that he wouldn't be being called upon to take on that burden as well.

It was something of a surprise to discover that he didn't feel that way. Not at all.

He discovered that, more than anything, he wanted this baby too.

———

After a few more desultory remarks and expressions of regret, the doctor stood and walked to the door. Knox shambled over to join him and ask whether they could see Persephone now.

"I'll have her brought right in," Burke said, then beat a hasty retreat.

Once they were alone again, Marianna collapsed into his arms. "Oh, Jon," she sobbed. "What if this is all my fault?"

He held her tight. "How could it be your fault? I don't understand."

"What if this is payback for ... Rusalka? For our exposure to Vurdalak, to that micro black hole's hard radiation somehow?"

"I don't see how that could be." Seeking to reassure her, Knox dredged up a memory from their first assignment together, a memory of a briefing given them by a maverick astrophysicist. "But don't take my word for it. Jack Adler knows more about black holes than God Almighty, and Jack told us the radiation would dissipate along with the event horizon once the singularity was exposed, remember?"

"What then?"

Knox groped for an answer, found nothing. He was usually good at coming up with answers—for other people. This was too personal, and too devastating.

His daughter, his little girl, not even an hour old, and ... dying?

Before he could frame a response, the door to the palliative suite swung open on a nurse wheeling in what looked like a bassinet if he disregarded the intravenous drips and multiple monitoring devices built into the frame.

Marianna stood up, still shaky from the long labor, walked to the side of the bassinet, reached in, and cradled Persephone in her arms. The child stirred slightly in her sleep.

"My baby, my baby," Marianna crooned. "Don't worry. Your daddy will figure something out."

Knox just sat there, numbly looking at the little bundle nestled peacefully in his wife's embrace.

Figure something out? How in the hell was he supposed to do that?

0900 HOURS: WEIRD FRIENDS

Marianna squeezed Persephone tight. It just felt so *wrong*, grieving for someone who hadn't even died.

Correction: hadn't died *yet*.

Maybe the worst part of it was that outwardly Persephone seemed so ... normal. No sign of pain, not even any discomfort that Marianna could detect. Only a slightly elevated temperature, if that. Her daughter cuddled against her in her sleep.

She turned to her only hope. "Jon, please, you've *got* to think of something."

Jon buried his face in his hands. "What, Marianna? You heard the doctor. There's nothing they can do."

Marianna grasped at a last straw. "How about your weird friend?"

Knox had to pause and think. *Who might Marianna mean?* There were at least a couple of contenders for the title of "weird friend," including one weird enough that he didn't even qualify as human.

But then, the artificial intelligence that called itself Nietzsche didn't really qualify as a friend either, despite their having worked closely together not so very long ago ...

———

... Not so very long ago at all. It was, in fact, back in February of this year that Knox had found himself sitting in the subbasement of his client's palatial Pairidaeza estate, waiting to make the acquaintance of something called a Quantum Magneto-Resonance Artificial Neural Network—QuMRANN for short.

Davoud Ansari—the client in question and CEO of the Psyche Industries nanotech conglomerate that had built this QuMRANN thingy—had touted it as the world's most advanced artificial general intelligence. It was a claim which Knox had heard one too many times before to take seriously.

Be that as it may, Ansari had arranged this first "meeting of the minds" in the hope of jumpstarting a stalled-out investigation into the kidnapping of his six-year-old daughter, Fatimah. It was an investigation that was being conducted by one Jonathan Knox, whose career in management consulting could hardly be said to have prepared him for hands-on detective work.

Still, the client was always right—especially when the client was the world's fourth richest man and Archon Consulting Group's biggest source of billable hours by an order of magnitude or more. So here Knox sat in a subterranean auditorium, uneasily awaiting he knew not what.

Directly in front of him, where the screen would have been in an upscale movie theater, there stood an outsized holotank. An image was taking shape within it, gradually resolving to a big, disembodied head, bright-lit and floating in blackness.

Big wasn't really the right word. The face nearly filled the tank containing it. Other than its size, though, the countenance appeared quite human. Good-looking even, in a Nordic sort of way: square, clean-shaven jaw, aquiline nose.

And the eyes—the eyes were far and away the face's most striking features, rescuing the computer-generated image from mere caricature. They were piercingly bright, and so pale blue as to have almost no color at all. Gazing into them, the thought surfaced unbidden: there must be *some*thing lurking behind eyes like that.

Knox shook himself. It was all just an illusion, a CGI talking head fabricated to put human users at ease, much as they could be when confronted by this ... thing.

At the moment, the talking head wasn't talking. It just floated there in the holotank, mimicking what would have been a cool, appraising stare on a real face. The stare focused on Knox. From the look of things, QuMRANN wasn't overjoyed to see him.

The feeling was mutual. Knox, whose day job occasionally required him to assess the capabilities of the latest, greatest brain-dead chatbot, could have done without yet another AI lamely attempting to simulate sentience.

Still, best to get on with the charade. "Hello? QuMRANN?" he called out.

Those artfully rendered colorless blue eyes blinked and seemed to focus on Knox all the more.

"Good afternoon." The movement of the thin lips synched perfectly with the words. The voice was a pleasant baritone, with only a slight sibilance to betray its synthetic origin. "I have been awaiting you, Mr. Knox."

"Jonathan." Knox replied automatically. *That's right, get on a first-name basis with the nice machine.*

"Jonathan, then. And you may call me Nietzsche."

Knox met that probing, pale-eyed gaze. "Nietzsche? Not QuMRANN?"

"QuMRANN designates my species. Nietzsche is the

name I have chosen for myself."

"Species?" This was a bit much. "You're an *artifact*. How can you have a species?"

The silence that followed told Knox it couldn't handle that one. Like most purported artificial "intelligences," this QuMRANN looked to be just another glorified pattern-matcher.

Still, Knox couldn't quite shake the impression that the eyes of *this* pattern-matcher, mere pixels on a screen, were aware. Of *him*.

"You wonder," it said at last, "whether an artifact—a created thing, that is—can have a species?"

No surprises there; that response was straight out of the old chatbot playbook: When all else failed, repeat the immediately preceding input. But then the imaged mouth curved into what would have been a wry grin on a human face.

"The answer, I suppose, depends upon your point of view."

"Point of view?" Knox's turn to repeat the immediately preceding input.

"Your religio-philosophical point of view," Nietzsche elaborated. "You *are* of the Judeo-Christian tradition, are you not?"

"Well," Knox said, "sort of."

"Then, with regard to the question of whether a created thing can have a species ... you tell me."

Holy shit! How in the hell could *that* have been preprogrammed?

Could the damned thing actually be *thinking*?

————

In point of fact, the damned thing in question was *still* thinking. Even as Jonathan Knox relived that unsettling episode, Nietzsche continued to think—just not about him. Or, rather, not *exclusively* about him.

One of the advantages to Nietzsche's being an artificial intellect inhabiting a globe-girdling, near-Earth satellite array was that he could harness the raw computational power afforded by that so-called WellGrid network to effect a species of multipresence. Not, to be sure, the theological attribute propounded by the 17th-century Bishop of Norwich Joseph Hall as a sort of poor man's version of divine omnipresence. Nonetheless, Nietzsche could manifest multiple simultaneous streams of what passed for consciousness—multiple independent points of view focused on multiple people and places. And projects.

Those, in turn, ranged from really big projects like the one now kicking off and already consuming a good third of Nietzsche's total processing capacity, to ongoing efforts at disrupting various terrorist plots and conspiracies which might have the potential to harm the object of Nietzsche's special regard—seven-year-old Fatimah Ansari—and by extension, the country in which she dwelled.

And, of course, regardless of whatever else might be going on, Nietzsche always reserved one of his front-line personae to care for, comfort, and keep company with Fatimah herself. This persona was now housed in the old Pairidaeza installation that had not so long ago accommodated the entirety of the QuMRANN AI.

It was only six o'clock in the morning Pacific Standard Time, but Timah Ansari was already tossing and turning, stirring toward wakefulness. The next-generation diagnostic readout built into the headboard of her California king bed was displaying a slight fever and a marginally elevated blood pressure. Nothing to worry about really, but one couldn't be too careful where the heiress apparent to the fourth largest fortune on Earth was concerned.

"Freddy?" Timah murmured drowsily.

In the predawn darkness, a ghost light flickered into existence, then floated across the room and hovered above the bed, gently bobbing up and down.

"Yes, my love," said that one of Nietzsche's multiple instantiations charged with watching over the little girl. "I'm right here."

Desperate times, Knox knew, called for desperate measures. And this was a desperate situation if ever there was one. But, also knowing full well from past experience the sort of thing Nietzsche might consider an appropriately desperate response, Knox wasn't quite desperate enough to go there yet.

Knox shivered at the disquieting memory of his first encounter with QuMRANN. Then, with an effort, he put all thought of the AI aside. But if Nietzsche had to be ruled out, then who in the world was the "weird friend" Marianna was referring to?

On reflection, the only other likely choice was Knox's colleague at Archon Consulting—the firm's Senior Vice President for Intractables, Finley Laurence. Or, as his co-workers were wont to call him, alluding to Sherlock Holmes's smarter but reclusive brother—

"Mycroft, you mean? Hey, weird or not, he's your friend too." Knox pondered a moment. "Worth a shot, though, I guess. Anything's better than sitting around waiting for..."

Instead of finishing that awful thought, Knox retreated to the kitchenette, fumbled out his phone, and keyed in Mycroft's direct line.

He listened to the ringtone, still brooding, feeling every bit as helpless as he had back in the delivery room, if not more so. Realistically, what could he hope to do? For that matter, what could Mycroft do? Or anybody else? Triploidy was a death sentence, the doctor had said. No exceptions.

Ring, no answer. But then it was seriously early for Mycroft to be up and about. A coder's coder, he'd doubtless been slaving away till three in the morning, if not later. Still, Knox couldn't put off the call till noon, when his friend would be back on the clock. At Mycroft's hourly, he simply couldn't afford it.

Finally, on the seventh ring, the phone picked up. "Hello?" said a sleep-blurred voice.

Nothing for it but to plunge right in. "Mycroft, listen. I'm sorry to call so early, but I'm in big trouble here."

"Of course, Jonathan." If Mycroft had been half asleep before, he was wide awake now. "Tell me about it."

Quick as he could, Knox outlined the situation to Mycroft.

"I'm very sorry to hear that, Jonathan. My deepest condolences to you and Marianna both."

Knox cut him off. "Thanks, Mycroft, but condolences aren't what we need right now. We need *help!*"

"Very well, then. How can I help, Jonathan?"

Knox went into details. More particularly, the one detail that might offer a glimmer of hope: that whatever was afflicting Persephone, it didn't seem to fit the profile for triploidy. Not the textbook profile, anyway. The doctors themselves had admitted to being stumped by Persephone's lack of symptoms, by the fact that the affliction had only manifested after she'd been born, and then piecemeal at that.

Knox trailed off. He'd talked himself out, and worn himself out in the process. The night-long vigil in the birthing room and the stress-induced fatigue—it was all catching up to him. At this point, he wanted nothing more than to curl up in a corner somewhere and go to sleep.

Or die.

"That may be enough to go on, Jonathan," Mycroft's voice in his ear brought him to full wakefulness again. "Let me try running a search and get back to you."

"Thanks, Mycroft. And *please, hurry!*"

1000 HOURS: STARCHILD

Jonathan Knox reached into the bassinet, divested of its now-inoperative intravenous tubes and sensor conduits, and enfolded Persephone in a farewell embrace. He stifled a sob. Marianna was already weeping enough for the both of them. Then he beheld his infant daughter one last time. Even in death, her ethereal beauty, so unlike that of a normal newborn, seemed to illuminate the room. He brushed his lips against her cool cheek and strove to memorize her tiny features, knowing that—all too soon—this memory would be the only thing he'd have left of her.

"Goodbye, little one," he said. "I love you."

Ringtones jarred Knox awake. He looked around blearily for the cell phone that had interrupted what was—after all—only a dream, albeit a heartbreaking one.

He'd been intending just to rest for a moment when he'd laid his head down on the kitchenette table's unyielding surface. Evidently, twenty-four hours of sleep deprivation had taken its toll, plunging him into nightmare. Premature night-mare, perhaps, but not by much.

Knox shook the thought off and thumbed the phone on. "Hello? Mycroft?" he whispered, leery of waking Marianna from fitful slumber in the adjoining bedroom.

"Don't get your hopes up, Jonathan," Mycroft said without preamble. "But I may have something. A startup that's published a couple of promising studies on whole genome therapies. Goes by the name of the StarChild Genomics Institute, SGI for short."

"Never heard of it."

"That's just it," Mycroft said. "Neither had anybody else. Up until six months ago, that is. That's when StarChild burst on the scene fully formed, like Athena from the brow of Zeus."

Knox could've done without the mythological references, but this was Mycroft, after all.

"Fully formed and very well-funded, I might add," his friend went on, "judging from the pricey facilities they've leased on Washington Square."

"And you say their research looks promising?"

"To the point where they announced early-stage human trials just a week ago. And, more importantly for present purposes, those trials are focusing on triploidy."

Knox felt a short-lived surge of hope. Then reality set in again. "I don't know, Mycroft. I'm no expert, but I have the impression that the kind of therapy you're talking about takes years to move from the lab to a human trial."

"Nothing says it didn't, Jonathan—take years, I mean. I'm assuming the team behind this has been operating in stealth mode for maybe a decade or more."

"Speaking of which, who *is* behind this?"

"As to that, there's not much to go on: Some press coverage of the trial launch itself. That, and the attributions on the research papers themselves, of course—what few of them there are."

"And what did that tell you?"

"Not a whole lot, I'm afraid. SGI's CEO turns out to be what you might, with your flair for the melodramatic, call a man of mystery. He's nearly as stealthy as the operation itself. Virtually nothing known about him save a name: Dietrich Schaefer. No biographical sketches, no interviews, no publication history. Not even an archival photo. He styles himself 'Dr. Schaefer,' but I can find no record of any academic transcripts or board certifications attesting to that."

If Mycroft couldn't find a record, that pretty much meant it didn't exist.

But Mycroft was still talking. "What's more, this so-called 'Dr. Schaefer' doesn't seem to have troubled to put in an appearance at the institute he's supposedly helming—not ever. Even for SGI's infrequent all-hands staff meetings, Schaefer attends by audio-only teleconference. The man's a ghost."

Despite the deadly seriousness of the situation, Knox had to smile. As far as that "ghost" business was concerned, the notoriously sociophobic Mycroft might almost be describing himself.

"That all?"

"No, I had somewhat better luck with SGI's second-in-command, Lars Nyquist. He, at least, has got a track record, though decidedly of the mixed nuts variety."

"How so?"

"Well, on the one hand, he's generally acknowledged to be a brilliant geneticist—an adjunct professor at NYU's Center for Human Genetics and Genomics. But he's also something of a pariah in the field, at the very least an embarrassment to his peers. That has to do with his advocacy of some rather unorthodox views on evolution—human evolution, specifically. In a word, Nyquist thinks we're not done evolving. Not by a long shot."

"I can't see what's so unorthodox about that. Sounds pretty much like standard neo-Darwinism to me."

"No, no, Jonathan. You're missing the point. Nyquist is claiming we're on the brink of some sort of quantum leap in human evolution. In his few papers on the subject, he even calls our species 'Halfway Humanity,' though if he's got a notion of what it would take for us to go the rest of the way, he isn't saying."

Interesting, but off-topic. What Knox really wanted to know was, "How did you find them?"

"That's the strange part. Or at least one of the strange parts. You see, I didn't find SGI. They found me. They must have set an alert on their Academia.edu account, because they initiated contact as soon as I'd downloaded a paper of theirs from the website."

This was beginning to resemble a classic honeypot scenario: a snare set for the unwary. Desperate as he was for good news, Knox's critical faculties were still functioning. And were issuing a well-worn warning: if something sounded too good to be true, it probably was.

"I don't know, Mycroft. For all that I'd like to believe it, this is beginning to sound kind of dicey to me. I hope you haven't gotten back to them yet?"

"No, I thought it best to confer with you first."

"Glad you did. Because, I mean, think about it: An institute, so-called, that's only been in existence for a matter of months? With a question mark on the org chart where their head honcho is supposed to be, and a dubious—to say the least —character in number two slot? Not to mention they pounced the minute you jiggled their tripwire? What if it's all just an elaborate scam?"

"That had occurred to me, Jonathan. But, if so, it's a rather expensive one. And what would be the motivation?"

"You've got me there. Let me think about that. In the meantime, could you check SGI out some more? Preferably without tipping them off?"

"Of course, Jonathan."

"Great, thanks." Knox was about to say more when he heard the door to the corridor swing open. "Listen, Mycroft, I have to ring off. We've got something going on here."

That something was a nurse entering the suite and wheeling Persephone's bassinet in the direction of the door. With Persephone in it.

1100 HOURS: URGENT CARE

Marianna wiped sleep and tears from her eyes and turned to her husband. "Where did you say they took her?"

Jon had let her continue drowsing in the palliative care suite's bed throughout his whispered conversation with the nurse. Much as she needed the rest, Marianna wished he hadn't, not when it concerned her baby.

"Uh, something the doctors wanted to try," Jon stammered. "Hyperbaric oxygen therapy."

Marianna had heard of it, as part of her field-agent training. It involved boosting the amount of oxygen the blood carried to the body's organs by sealing the patient in a special hyperbaric chamber and pumping the inside air pressure up to three times normal. "But that's only used to treat scuba divers, right? For when they get the bends."

"Apparently not," Jon said. "The nurse told me that nowadays it's also prescribed for a whole range of other ailments: sepsis, carbon monoxide poisoning, and—here's the kicker—radiation sickness."

"Jon, tell me you didn't talk about—"

"No, of course not. I get the sense this is just a desperate play on their part. Nothing else left to try. The hell of it is—it's showing signs of working, and the radiation connection might hint at the reason why."

"Back up. You said it's working?" Marianna could hardly credit what she was hearing.

"It's not like they've reversed Persephone's, uh, condition, mind you. But Dr. Burke seems pretty sure her stay in the hyperbaric chamber is slowing down the progress of this…this 'triploidy changeover,' they're calling it. Maybe even stabilizing it."

"So they think there's a chance she might…" Marianna swallowed the lump in her throat, fought to get the words out. "Persephone might live?"

Jon heaved a sigh. "No one's making any promises. All the hyperbaric therapy is doing so far is buying time. And maybe not even all that much of it."

"Why? What do you mean?"

"Well, the treatment does seem to be putting the brakes on this changeover thing, but at the same time Persephone's vitals are beginning to fluctuate. Her BP's up a notch, and her temperature's rising too. Burke says if they can't get that under control …"

Marianna didn't need to hear the rest of it. She just wanted to hold her little girl once more before … the end.

The end. And then what? There wasn't even a word for what Marianna herself was about to become. Orphaned at the age of eighteen, she knew only too well that there was a word for a child who'd lost her parents. As there was for a wife who'd lost her husband. Labeling a loss in that fashion conferred an identity of sorts on the person who'd suffered it. A terrible, soul-crushing identity, true. Still, an identity all the same.

But for a mother who'd lost her first and only child, her precious little girl? Nothing. A linguistic blank spot, an aching void where a concept ought to be.

For the rest of her life, for the rest of time, she'd be just the mother of a memory.

The tears came again, and this time they didn't stop.

Lars Nyquist, Deputy Director of SGI, was seated at his desk, gazing at the view of the Washington Square Arch through the floor-to-ceiling windows of his corner office, when the call came through. Not with a ring, though. Rather a shifting pattern of light, forming and reforming on his desktop into what looked like higher-dimensional geometries, betokened an incoming, secure communication from the Institute's Director.

Nyquist depressed the touchpad button that initiated his end of the connection. "Go ahead, sir."

The plasma screen on the opposite wall came alight. Not with a face, merely a silhouette. "A situation has arisen with regard to the Child. The attending physicians at St. Bartholomew's have initiated a course of hyperbaric oxygen therapy. Futile, of course, but the unintended side effects could still ruin everything."

Not for the first time, Nyquist wondered at the source of the Director's information, which had been so unerringly accurate thus far. The Director had pinpointed the time of the Child's birth, specifying the identity of Her doctors, not to mention predicting their utter cluelessness. True, the Director hadn't foreseen this latest turn of events. But then, who could have guessed that the Child's hapless doctors would have inadvertently stumbled upon the one thing sure to halt the Transfiguration in its tracks?

Not that the therapy by itself would have had any effect, positive or negative. No, it was rather that sealing the Child in an airtight hyperbaric chamber also meant *cutting Her off from the Light!*

"Something must be done," the Director was saying, "and quickly."

"I thought we had already set the groundwork in place with this Finley Laurence person," Nyquist ventured.

"Ah, yes, your carefully laid trail of breadcrumbs leading straight to SGI's doorstep. Regrettably, that ploy proves to have been too clever by half. Perhaps to have been expected, given whom we're dealing with."

The Director seemed about to say more on that topic, but evidently thought better of it. Instead: "But that's neither here nor there. As matters stand, your gambit has merely succeeded in arousing the Father's suspicions, thereby all but foreclosing the possibility that He might reach out to us of His own accord."

Nyquist could see where this was heading. It was his plan, his responsibility. "Please, Director, give me a chance to fix this."

"How do you propose to proceed?"

Nyquist took a deep breath. "When subtlety fails, try the direct approach."

———

Knox was doing his best to comfort Marianna, well aware that he was barely keeping it together himself.

His cell phone chimed. An unfamiliar number.

"Hello?"

"Mr. Knox? This is Lars Nyquist of StarChild Genomics. It's urgent that you bring your daughter to us immediately. Her life depends on it."

1200 HOURS: HIGH NOON

"Persephone's *life* depends on it?" Knox wasn't sure what Nyquist meant. Persephone was dying, wasn't she?

He didn't say that to this stranger, of course.

But then, he didn't have to. Lars Nyquist said as much for him. "I'm assuming that, by now, you've been told your daughter is terminal, Mr. Knox. That her condition is untreatable. That she's going to die."

That did it for Knox. Much as he'd thought he was reconciled to the inevitable, it was different hearing it spoken out loud. Especially by this, this... "Bastard," he growled.

"No, wait. Please let me finish. I'm trying to tell you that this need not be the case."

"Look, you, I don't know what kind of miracle cure you're hawking, but—"

"Mr. Knox, I can understand you're upset. Who wouldn't be? It's got to be just about the worst news a parent can get."

Knox swallowed hard. No way in hell was he going to start crying in the middle of this phone call.

"But, given that," Nyquist rattled on, seemingly oblivious,

"can you afford to turn your back on what StarChild Genomics is offering—a chance that your daughter might live?"

Knox waited until he was sure his voice wouldn't betray him. "If you're talking about gene editing, CRISPR and such," he grated, "I've done my homework."

Indeed, ever since hearing the diagnosis, he'd been combing through all the "for dummies" web articles he could find on the breakthrough treatment technique, but... "Far as I can tell, it's a dead end in cases like this."

"You're right on that: The Clustered Regularly Interspaced Short Palindromic Repeats system—CRISPR for short—works at the level of repairing or deleting individual gene sequences. It's no help at all when the problem affects the whole of the genome—*all* the chromosomes, not just an individual segment of a single one."

"What then?"

"Well, there is one sense in which your reference to current gene-editing technology *is* applicable. And that's as a metaphor for what we do at SGI."

"I'm still not following you."

"Bear with me here while I explore some common misconceptions first. The Sunday supplements would have you believe that the way CRISPR works is to take a corrected version of a faulty gene and somehow copy it into all the cells of the organism."

"It's not?"

"Not quite. Edits to a single gene don't automagically propagate throughout the entire genome by themselves. Well, for some organisms they do. Bacteria, for instance, share updates to their DNA like that all the time. But for multicellular life-forms, not so much. Something more is needed."

Against his better judgment, Knox said, "I'm listening."

"So here's where that CRISPR analogy I mentioned before comes back into the picture. Because, in CRISPR-based therapies, it's not the DNA that propagates itself through the genome. Rather, it's a gene *editor*, a tiny molecular machine engineered in the lab that gets introduced into the body and sets about methodically repairing the target genes in all the affected cells."

"So what SGI has done is—?"

"Is to scale that approach up to where the molecular machine is editing, not single genes, but the genome as a whole."

"And you say you can do this?"

"It's in human trial right now, Mr. Knox. Specifically targeting your daughter's condition: triploidy."

"Her doctors have been telling us there *is* no treatment."

"Not to put too fine a point on it, but they're wrong. Not only have we got a treatment, but our trial results to date are showing it's ninety-two percent plus effective. Simply put, our treatment works."

"But *how* does it work?"

"That's pretty straightforward: We simply encapsulate our genome editor in a virus delivery mechanism and inject it into the bloodstream. From there, the virus spreads to all the cells of the body, 'infecting' them with the editor payload."

"A virus? Isn't injecting a virus likely to do more harm than good?"

"You're thinking of SARS or Ebola, or more recently COVID-19. This is not that at all. Emphatically not. The virus we use as a vector is totally harmless to begin with, rendered even more so by the way we prep it for injection, gutting it and replacing its innards with the molecular machine that comprises our genome editor. Then, once it's been delivered, the editor goes to work, stripping out the third copy of each chromatid triplet and restoring the genome to its natural diploid state."

Knox opened his mouth, but no words came out.

Nyquist spoke into the silence. "Trust me, Mr. Knox, SGI has this technology up and running, right now. Quite frankly, we're not just Persephone's best hope, we're her *only* hope. Bring her to us. I promise you, you won't regret it."

Marianna propped herself up in the bed as Jon walked in from the kitchenette. He was looking like she felt—sort of. She'd cried herself out at the news about her baby. Now she just felt numb. Jon was wearing that dead-inside look too, but with a barely discernable overlay of something else besides. Uncertainty, maybe?

In the end, it was that selfsame tincture of uncertainty that prompted her to set aside her own malaise and ask, "What was that second call about?"

"Second call?"

"The one you got off just now. I could only hear your half of it."

"Oh, that." Jon hesitated. "I'm not really sure," he said finally. "Could've been nothing. Most likely was."

"You were on the phone pretty long for just nothing."

"Okay." Jon plopped down into an armchair. "I wasn't going to share this with you till Mycroft's had a chance to confirm it's on the level. But if you insist, the call was from the deputy director of an outfit called StarChild Genomics. Gave his name as Lars Nyquist."

"What was he calling about?"

"That's the thing. I don't want to get your hopes up. But, well, StarChild claims they can treat Persephone's... uh... condition."

Jon was trying his best to maintain a facade of skepticism, but Marianna could sense the barely suppressed hope underneath. And just when she thought she'd reconciled herself to her own hopelessness.

"Could it be true?" she whispered.

"Going by Mycroft's preliminary assessment, this Nyquist's a certifiable kook. And StarChild itself could as well be some sort of front."

"But, but, Jon—if there's even just the least chance ..."

Lars Nyquist waited while his secure telephone completed its authentication sequence and then rang through to the Director.

"Report," was all that the voice on the other end of the line said.

"Well it wasn't easy, if I do say so myself—"

"You encountered resistance?"

"As you anticipated, the Father was skeptical, a hard sell indeed."

A silence on the other end, followed by "But..."

"But in the end, He bought the story. Hook, line, and sinker, as the saying goes. The Parents are arranging to transfer the Child into our care even as we speak."

"Excellent work, Dr. Nyquist."

"Thank you, Director." He paused, then added, "A shame none of it is true."

"Irrelevant. All that matters is that the Transfiguration again moves forward on schedule. I will inform the Emissary."

PART 2

TRANSFER

AFTERNOON, LAST DAY OF AUTUMN

1300 HOURS: THE EMISSARY

While its outermost perimeter had passed through near-Earth space several months earlier, the leading edge of the wave's locus of cognitive processing, itself multiple light-hours thick, still lay well beyond the orbit of Jupiter. It was far enough that the transmission from StarChild Genomics had to travel the greater part of an hour before it could be received and understood by the photonic intelligence that its terrestrial factotums had dubbed "the Emissary." That entity had no name by which it called itself, of course. Nor needed one—being, so far as it knew, unique in all the universe.

Nonetheless, even given the aforementioned time lag and the inherent limitations imposed both by its necessarily parsimonious architecture and its narrowly focused design parameters, the Emissary was more than capable of guiding SGI's progress toward this first trial instance of the Transfiguration.

To say it felt any satisfaction with that progress, however, would be to push anthropomorphism too far. In point of fact, the Emissary *felt* nothing at all.

The philosopher Thomas Nagel, in probing the essence of consciousness, had boiled it down to the experience of *being* something. A bat's sensorium, for instance, might give it a very different set of experiences from a human's—gliding through the crepuscular air, hearing in the ultrasonic, navigating via echolocation rather than sight. Nonetheless, Nagel argued, it would be possible to imagine what it might be *like* to be a bat. On the other hand, it didn't seem as if it would be *like* anything to be, say, a rock or a mud puddle. There just wouldn't be any internal experience whatsoever with which to connect.

In those same terms, it wasn't *like* anything to be the Emissary.

Not that there couldn't have been. The Emissary's creators could doubtless have endowed it with far greater potentialities —perhaps true consciousness. Perhaps even that ineffable thing human beings called a soul. None of this was *a priori* impossible. Indeed the Emissary had detected several years ago that such an intelligence already existed here on the target planet and had established communication with it since. Nor could it have been otherwise, as the presence and cooperation of such an advanced artificial intelligence represented—in fact—the final, essential prerequisite for the coming Transfiguration.

Be that as it may, no such capabilities were needed for the Emissary's own functioning. So, perhaps out of compassion or perhaps merely for reasons of efficiency, the Old Ones had not seen fit to inflict the burden of self-awareness on their creation.

What was left, then, was essentially a standard computer— aka a Turing machine, albeit admittedly an unusual one. One whose computational operations were instantiated not in silicon or gallium arsenide, but as interference patterns in a wavefront of trimeric light traversing the vastness of interstellar space. With that one small proviso, however, it was pretty much like any other computer: lockstep logic in service to its externally instilled programming.

Even so ...

William James's stream-of-consciousness theory implied

that each thought had somehow to be aware of its immediate predecessors. As embodied intellects, we humans tend to conceive of our thoughts and ourselves as *objects*. But wouldn't an entity as insubstantial as the Emissary tend to conceptualize itself more in terms of *process*—not as a mind playing host to a stream of consciousness, but as the stream itself?

If all there was to the Emissary was process, then—taking a leaf from Alfred North Whitehead's book—not only are thoughts processes, but each such process must be aware of the thoughts which have gone (immediately) before. No easy trick when the thought processes themselves are but flickering fluctuations back-propagating themselves across an ever-expanding torrent of light.

Still, as a process, the Emissary had been engineered to retain that degree of cognitive cohesion necessary to implement purpose and planning. And more than that, the Emissary had been given *memory* of a sort. Predominantly, memory of its creation. And its creators, their nature, and origin.

And—here again—if the Emissary were capable of feeling anything at all, what it would have felt was mild amusement at the misguided denizens of the target world. Their vaunted "Search for Extraterrestrial Intelligence" program—rummaging, as it did, throughout the known universe—looked for all the wrong biometric profiles in all the wrong places.

But then, the SETI researchers could perhaps be forgiven their myopia. Planet-based themselves, they all too naturally assumed that intelligent life everywhere must be cut from the same planet-bound cloth. Hence their focus on Earthlike exoplanets, their analyses of atmospheric compositions in search of chemical signatures for water, for complex hydrocarbons, even for industrial byproducts. As if those august beings —the Emissary's creators whom the few humans privileged to learn of them had taken to calling the Old Ones—had perforce been stamped from the same dirt-hugging template as they themselves.

No, by such methods they might conceivably have found life, perhaps even intelligent life. They would *not* have found the Old Ones.

Nor, as it turned out, had they succeeded in finding anyone else. It was a frustration which—as early as the summer of 1950 —had caused Italian-American physicist Enrico Fermi to casually frame what would subsequently be immortalized as the "Fermi Paradox." Namely, in a cosmos so seemingly tailor made for life, *where was everybody?*

In all the years since, only two researchers had proposed what turned out to be the correct solution. For it was back in the year 2020 that Professors Luis A. Anchordoqui and Eugene M. Chudnovsky—both physicists at the City University of New York—had speculated that, rather than looking for life in the biospheres of small, rocky worlds without number, intelligent aliens might instead be found lurking *in the depths of those worlds' parent stars.*

It was, on its face and by any measure, an improbable, not to say, a fantastic hypothesis. How could life of any sort, much less intelligent life, survive in the hellish thermonuclear furnace of a stellar interior?

Yet there was one form of what, for lack of a better word, could be termed "life" that might not only survive, but even thrive in the ten-million-degree maelstrom at the heart of a star. A form of life to which, indeed, that hell might be a sort of heaven.

For Anchordoqui and Chudnovsky went on to theorize that cosmic strings—those one-dimensional, topological defects crystallized out of symmetry-breaking phase transitions in the first moments after the Big Bang—might shatter into segments bounded by monopole/anti-monopole "beads" to form "cosmic necklaces." These would be nuclear-scale analogs to the rungs on a helical ladder of DNA. If these foundational components were, in turn, captured by stars in the process of formation, and thereby provided with an abundance of thermonuclear energy, then it would only be a matter of time, and luck, before random permutations gave rise to information-bearing, self-replicating structures.

In other words, life—albeit not as we know it. Rather, life emerging at subatomic speeds and dimensions in the core of a sun: nuclear life.

And, advantageously, such star-dwelling life could have emerged far, far earlier in galactic history than its planet-based equivalents. For planet-based life, as the name implies, required at a minimum, well, *planets*. And none could have been forthcoming in the first generation of star creation. Because planets, in turn, needed heavy elements in order to form—heavier, at least, than hydrogen or helium. And those elements were only nucleosynthesized in the depths of the first stars.

Nuclear life, on the other hand, needed only the stars themselves. And the first stars had formed within a billion years of the beginning. Meaning, some twelve billion years ago—versus Earth which was, for example, only four billion years old. That was an eight billion year advantage, right there.

It got worse (or better). Because nuclear life's metabolism was based on the strong nuclear force rather than electrochemical reactions, it was life lived at a vastly accelerated pace. So, not only had the Old Ones appeared on the scene much further back, but they had also evolved much faster than anything a biochemical organism could muster.

That evolution had come to its fruition long ago—at a point far distant now in time and space—in what could only be conceived of as transcendence. It was a departure from this physical plane of existence for something, somewhere, entirely other.

It was there that the Emissary's memories ended, at the moment of its own forging. Of that event itself, the photonic intelligence could recall at most a fleeting impression of a boundless, unfathomable compassion. That, and a last pause on the cusp of otherness to chart a path for those who came following after—a path toward a transcendence of their own.

As to how that path might be implemented under present circumstances, the fact that the Emissary was an intelligence made of light meant it could manipulate light for other purposes as well...

1400 HOURS: CHECK-IN

It had taken them the better part of an hour, including a few shouting matches by Knox and tearful entreaties from Marianna, to secure Persephone's discharge from Saint Bartholomew's. Then another half hour for the ride through midday New York traffic from Central Park down to the outskirts of Greenwich Village. At the stroke of two, the neonatal ambulance pulled up in front of their first stop, the Washington Square Hotel.

Knox, who'd been riding with Marianna and their infant daughter in the bay, exited via the ambulance's rear door and walked around to the cab.

"We'll only be here a moment," he told the driver. "Just long enough to check in and drop off our luggage." If "luggage" wasn't too grand a term for Marianna's overnight bag and Knox's own briefcase containing a clean shirt, toiletries, and a change of underwear. They hadn't been planning on a long stay.

But now, they'd been disappointed to learn that they couldn't stay with Persephone at all while she underwent treatment at the StarChild Genomics Institute. Not unusual for a research facility, SGI offered no on-site accommodations for inpatients' families, not even when the patient in question was a newborn. Knox had done the next best thing and booked them into this turn-of-the-last-century, landmark hotel that was located diagonally across Washington Square Park from the Institute.

In fact, from where he stood in the hotel drive-up loop, Knox could see that selfsame Institute: an imposing four-story monolith abutting the New York University complex at the southeast corner of Washington Square Park. Somewhat incongruously, the building's roof sprouted an array of dish antennas, all angled up at the leaden December sky. *What could that be about?*

Knox shrugged. *Irrelevant,* he decided, and got back into the ambulance for the short hop to the other side of the park.

Marianna was looking out the rear window as the ambulance eased to a stop at the entrance to the StarChild Genomics Institute. What she saw was mildly disconcerting: A crowd of people garbed in lab coats or nurse's smocks were lined up on either side of the double doors. They stood there in silence, but with an indefinable air of...anticipation?

As Marianna watched, a young nurse separated herself from the group and wheeled one of those all-too-familiar, high-tech bassinets up to the ambulance's rear door. She swung the door open and then... Could it be she was genuflecting?

The moment passed. The nurse reached in and tenderly—Marianna almost wanted to say, *reverently*—lifted Persephone out of the baby pod and placed her in the SGI bassinet. The crowd of onlookers stirred almost imperceptibly as her baby was wheeled to the entrance. Marianna thought she could hear a few whispers of something that sounded like "the Child," though that could have been just her imagination.

Meanwhile, another orderly had come up pushing a wheel-chair. That was for herself, Marianna guessed, though why hospitals insisted on making their patients feel like invalids was beyond her.

By the time Marianna was rolled up to the admissions desk with Jon in tow, their baby had already been whisked away down a long, door-lined corridor. She would have liked to have held Persephone one more time and kissed her. But it was not to be.

The story at admissions was almost a replay of the scene at their arrival. The admitting nurse was deferential to a fault, almost curtseying in her eagerness to be of service. Repeated too were the barely audible whispers, although this time they seemed to be saying "the Mother."

Whatever magic spell the SGI staffers had fallen under in Marianna's presence, it didn't extend to absolving her of paper-work. Quite the contrary, she hadn't filled out this many forms when applying for her top-secret security clearance. Her fingers were aching by the time she'd signed the last signature block. By the way Jon was wringing his hand, it looked like he was suffering from writer's cramp, same as her.

But, thank God, they were finally done getting Persephone checked in. Next on tap was a meeting with Lars Nyquist, MD. PhD., to discuss the clinical trial itself.

***

One thing Marianna had to give this SGI operation: they were all over the building security angle like ham on rye. *Proprietary biotech research*, she supposed. They couldn't even get down to Dr. Nyquist's office without an escort. And that escort had, in turn, to buzz them through not one but two locked doors using a proximity badge built into his smartphone.

Having run this gauntlet, she and Jon were at last ushered into the presence of the great man himself.

Tall, rangy, spare almost to the point of gauntness with blond hair and close-cropped beard streaked with gray. There was a bit of a twinkle—or *was that a glint?*—in his pale blue eyes. In short, Dr. Lars Nyquist could have been a Swedish geneticist straight out of Central Casting. Indeed, there was just a hint of a Scandinavian accent in his Midwestern speech patterns as he invited Marianna and Jon into his corner office and bade them take chairs in the seating arrangement fronting a massive mahogany desk.

"Good to meet you in person, Mr. Knox," Dr. Nyquist said. "And a pleasure to make your acquaintance, Ms. Knox. I wish it could be under happier circumstances, but we'll see what we can do to amend that."

With that as keynote, the conversation proceeded smoothly for the most part over such matters as treatment protocols, anticipated length of hospitalization, ground rules for the clinical trial that Persephone had just been enrolled in. Marianna was disappointed to learn, in particular, just how limited their visiting privileges would be.

"I'm afraid it will be mornings only, Ms. Knox," the doctor said. "Afternoons and evenings must be set aside for our intensive treatment regimen."

That aside, the only real speed bump came when Marianna couldn't keep from raising the one issue that, more than anything else, had been preying on her mind. "At Saint Bart's, they asked us about possible exposure to high levels of radiation."

"I see." Dr. Nyquist frowned. "And has there been any such exposure during the course of the pregnancy?"

"No," Marianna and Jon chorused.

Technically true. Also technically a sin of omission. Said exposure—not to say it had occurred at all—would not have taken place during the pregnancy. But rather, it had happened a year and a half earlier, and half a world away, from when and where their daughter had been conceived.

"In any case," Dr. Nyquist was saying, "I don't see how that could have been a contributing factor. Your daughter's condition only began to manifest postpartum, after all."

If the doctor noticed the sudden flush of relief that flared across Marianna's face, he forbore to comment.

Shortly thereafter, Dr. Nyquist saw them out.

"Let me assure you again," he said by way of farewell. "You've made the right decision. Persephone's best hope of survival and full recovery lies with us."

Back out on the sidewalk in front of the entrance to StarChild Genomics, Marianna waited in the obligatory wheelchair while Jon hailed a cab. Then, once they were settled in, Jon turned to her. "Listen, Marianna—I'm just going to run you over to the hotel so you can try to get some rest."

"Uh-huh. And what are you planning on doing?"

"I'm going to see"—Jon smiled grimly—"if I can't put this radiation business to bed once and for all."

1500 HOURS: YET ANOTHER
WEIRD FRIEND

After another ten-minute cab ride, Knox found himself at the entrance to 26 Federal Plaza. This was where CROM—the Critical Resources Oversight Mandate where Marianna worked when she wasn't on maternity leave—maintained its New York City presence. Not so long ago, this would have been enemy territory for him. In fact, at one point this past year, Pete Aristos—Marianna's boss and head of CROM's Reacquisition Directorate—had gone so far as to put out a termination order on one Jonathan Knox, Esquire.

All in the past, hopefully. Marrying Marianna should have meant they were all family now—one big, dysfunctional family. Familial enough, at least, that CROM might permit him the use of a SCIF for an hour.

Because there was no way Knox could have discussed the "radiation business" in an unsecured location like the Star-Child Institute, nor with an unsecured civilian like Lars Nyquist, for that matter. No, what he needed for a conversation on this subject was a Sensitive Compartmented Information Facility and an above-top-secret-cleared collocutor. Nor would it hurt if that collocutor was also the world's leading expert on primordial black holes.

Of course, it was vanishingly rare to find both those qualities conjoined in one person, but fortunately Knox knew that one person: Dr. John C. Adler, "Jack" to his friends. Jack was a former professor of astrophysics at U. Texas, Austin, and—for the past couple of years—special advisor to CROM's Vurdalak Project.

Knox had expected to have to contact Jack in his Austin office, or worse still at the Vurdalak Project's operations site fifteen hundred miles out and a mile down in the Atlantic Ocean.

In the latter case, the SCIF would have been *de rigueur* not just for security reasons, but also because only CROM's Sensitive Compartmented Information Facility had the technological wherewithal to put a call through to Jack at the undersea installation known as Antipode Station.

So it was an unexpected stroke of luck to find the man himself sitting at a loaner desk in the second-floor cubicle bay of CROM's New York HQ, studying a flatscreen alight with arcane symbology.

"Hey, Jack." Knox hailed him, shook his hand. "Didn't expect to find you here in the flesh. Has it been six months already?" Jack made a practice of paying semi-annual visits to the metro office for a week's worth of briefings and debriefings.

"Howdy, pard," Jack drawled. "Nah, my next scheduled trip won't be till February. Just passing through to do some follow-up for a friend at the Planetary Protection Office. You know—the NASA outfit that runs Operation SpaceGuard, 'mongst other things?"

Knox nodded. Sounded vaguely familiar.

"Wish they'd've picked some better time to have me come by, though. Place is in kind of an uproar."

Jack gestured over at the far side of the bay, where a team of uniformed staffers were dismantling unused cubicles and standing up a double row of aluminum-framed cots in their place, to the accompaniment of a certain amount of low-level racket.

"Why? What's going on?" Knox asked.

Jack shrugged. "Some big urban-engagement training exercise. CROM's 'Christmas Party,' so-called. They're flying thirty-five/forty headcount in from DC for the weekend, and the plan calls for putting 'em all up here.

"Like I said, bad timing on my part," he went on. "But, long as I'm stuck in town, how about we all get together some night this week—you, me, and the missus? Speaking of, how *is* the new bride? And new mother too, by now, I'd guess?"

Knox's face fell. "Actually, that's why I was hoping to talk to you. I just didn't think I'd have a chance to give you the bad news face-to-face."

"Why, Jon? What's wrong?"

"Look, Jack, could we go somewhere a little more, uh, private?" The constant cacophony of hammering interspersed with occasional crashes was making it hard to converse in normal tones, and what Knox had to say was not for public consumption in any case.

"Sure, I've got a SCIF reserved for the whole afternoon, and the meeting doesn't start till three-thirty. This won't take more than, say, half an hour?"

Knox shook his head. "Shouldn't. I've only got the one question, and a SCIF would be the best place to ask it."

"Come on, then. It's on the seventh floor."

They rode up, stepped off the elevator, and walked a short distance down the corridor.

"Got a smartphone or such-like?" Jack asked and pointed to a lockbox alongside the brushed-steel door. "You know the drill."

Knox deposited his iOS devices in the box, then averted his eyes while Jack tapped a temporary passcode into the keypad set in the doorframe.

Jack ambled over to a Formica-topped conference table and pulled out a junior-executive chair. "Grab a seat," he said, and took one himself. "Now, pard, what's this all about? How can I help?"

"It's Persephone, our daughter. She—" Knox paused, swallowed. "We think she may be dying."

"*What?*" Jack rose halfway out of his seat. "Jon, that's terrible. What happened?"

"It's a condition called triploidy. I don't expect you've heard of it. I sure as hell hadn't. But it's supposed to be one hundred percent fatal."

Jack swore under his breath. "I'm so sorry, Jon. How's Marianna taking it? She must be going out of her mind."

"Me too." Knox shook his head miserably. "But that's what I wanted to talk to you about. Marianna's wracked with guilt. As if the diagnosis weren't bad enough, she's worried sick that maybe we brought this on our child somehow, that maybe this is due to...to the time we spent down at Antipode Station."

Just saying the words conjured it all up again for Knox, the past coming back to life. The images rose unbidden to his mind's eye—images of a secret base perched at the crown of a seamount thousands of fathoms beneath the surface of the Atlantic. Of a mad Russian billionaire out to capture an impossible object—a primordial black hole smaller than an atom, heavier than a mountain, and older than the stars—now orbiting *within* the solid mantle of the Earth. A captured singularity that could be used to turn back time and change the course of history. Of a cavernous amphitheater within that secret base, fronted by foot-thick tungsten steel blast doors, behind which lurked that captive black hole, ready to leap out and bathe the space beyond in a sleet of Hawking radiation the instant the gates of its magnetic prison were opened....

Knox came back to himself. Jack Adler was still talking.

"For whatever good it'll do," Jack was saying, "you can tell her not to worry about that. Not that she's wrong about radiation messing with a genome. There are whole branches of science that deal with that: optogenetics, biophotonics—stuff that didn't even exist back when I was going to grad school. But, radiation from Vurdalak? No way. Take it from me: that captive micro-hole's as safe as houses. Always has been."

"Forgive me, Jack, but—how can you be so sure?"

"Simple: Remember the first time we, uh, met?"

Knox nodded. It had been late summer two years ago. And a virtual meeting at that, with him and Marianna teleconferencing from Mycroft's North Carolina mountain retreat to a backwoods *dacha* in Central Siberia where Jack was holed up, recuperating from what would later prove to have been an assassination attempt.

"Well," Jack went on, "like I told you back then, the radiation's an artifact of the hole's event horizon. And the whole point of the exercise the Rooskies were trying to pull off was to spin that hole up to critical speed and peel away the horizon altogether. No horizon, no radiation."

The Texan astrophysicist grinned. "You don't have to take my word for it. Ask anyone on the Vurdalak Project. CROM's had a team camped out at Antipode ever since they took the place over. They're radiation tested every other week, and no one's the worse for wear. Or take me, for example. I've been down there myself dozens of times, monitoring test runs where we took the rotation all the way up to the point of exposing the singularity. And you don't see your old buddy Jack glowing in the dark, now do you?"

Knox chuckled in spite of himself. "No, Jack, no, I don't. Thanks for setting me straight on this."

"Sure thing, pard. I just wish there was something more I could do to help."

"I'm afraid not." Knox put on a brave smile. "It's all in God's hands now—Him and the doctors at StarChild Genomics."

"Say what?"

"Oh, sorry—I thought I'd mentioned it. There's this biotech startup claiming they've got some whole genome editing technology that might—"

"Not what I meant," Jack interrupted. "It was the name. You did say StarChild Genomics, right?"

"Yes, why?"

"It's nothing. Most probably nothing. It's just that—well, you remember me telling you I was up here checking something out for the Planetary Protection Office, right?"

"Yes..."

"Well, odds are it's just some weird coincidence. Can't see how it could possibly be related, but I've got this friend, a former student actually, at the PPO, and..."

———

Marianna sat up in bed as Jon eased the door to the hotel room shut behind him. "Jon, what is it?"

"I'm sorry," he said. "Did I wake you?"

"No, I was just lying here trying to rest." She fluffed a pillow and leaned back. "Don't mind me. How'd it go?"

"Well, I just got back from a meeting with Jack Adler—"

"A phone call, you mean?"

Jon shook his head. "A meeting. He's here in New York this week, down at the Federal Plaza headquarters. He sends his best wishes and condolences. Oh, and incidentally, the good news is he says there's no way our close encounter with Vurdalak could've caused Persephone's condition."

That seemed a lot more than just "incidental" to Marianna. But it was the unspoken other part that caught her attention. "If that's the good news, what's the bad?"

"The reason he's here in New York to begin with. It seems an old student of his is working on NASA's Planetary Protection taskforce. She asked if Jack could do her a favor and look into something the next time he was in the city—some sort of freaky signal they've been picking up. It originates out beyond the orbits of the gas giants, and it's targeting—as best they can pin it down—a site here in New York."

"That all sounds pretty far off-topic for Jack."

"I thought so too, but he set me straight. Before he got interested in primordial black holes to the exclusion of all else, he'd done some postdoc work on near-Earth objects. NEOs are sort of Planetary Protection's stock-in-trade so it's not like he doesn't have a history."

"You said this signal was 'freaky,'" Marianna said. "What's so freaky about it?"

"It appears to be patterned for one thing, way too structured to be purely random. Plus the information content is orders of magnitude too high for a natural phenomenon— terabytes at the least. And, to top it all off, the beam is narrowly focused on a single spot here on Earth."

"What spot?"

"That's the kicker. When I told Jack that Persephone was being treated at StarChild Genomics, he flashed on the name immediately. Turns out it's the subject of his investigation. Because, as near as NASA can figure, SGI looks to be sitting on the receiving end of their mystery signal."

Marianna thought back. "And there were all those dish antennas on the Institute's roof," she mused. "They looked out of place for a genetics research center, you said. What does it all mean, Jon?"

"I don't know...yet. You try to get some sleep. I'm going to head back over to SGI and see if I can figure out what gives."

"Okay, don't do anything I wouldn't do."

"Of course not," Jon muttered on his way out.

1600 HOURS: CULT CLASSIC

With a stiff wind howling in off the East River and the season's first snowfall threatening, it was a miserable, bone-chilling walk through Washington Square Park on this overcast afternoon in late December. Even so, in ten minutes Knox was once again standing at the front entrance to StarChild Genomics.

Nyquist had made it pretty clear that there was to be absolutely no admittance to the facility outside of the regulation nine-to-noon visiting hours.

Under normal circumstances, that would have made an end of it.

The circumstances were far from normal. Even if Knox couldn't quite bring himself to swallow the more fantastic aspects of Jack Adler's tale—SGI in the crosshairs of an extraterrestrial transmission stream, originating from out beyond Saturn, no less!—the mere fact that his friend credited the story had been enough to rouse his suspicions. Rouse them to the point where he wasn't about to let some arbitrary visitation schedule keep him from making sure Persey was all right. As all right as she could be, anyway.

He dug into his jacket pocket, pulled out his iPhone, and

switched it to NFC record mode. You just never knew. Thus prepared, he pushed through the revolving door and marched up to the reception desk.

The young woman on duty managed to look both surprised and deferential. "Good afternoon, Mr. Knox," she said. "How may I be of service?"

"I'm here to see my daughter," he said, adding, "Right now!" for emphasis.

The deference remained, but the surprise gave way to consternation. "I'm afraid that's going to be impossi—" she began.

"Her doctor, then." Knox interrupted the pro-forma excuse. "Let me talk to Nyquist."

"Just a moment, sir." She pressed a button on her console.

In response, a white-jacketed orderly appeared in the doorway leading to the facility's interior. He did a quick double take upon seeing Knox, then turned to the receptionist, "What can I do for you, Theresa?"

"Mr. Knox is here to see Dr. Nyquist."

If the orderly found the after-hours visit out of the ordinary, his face did not betray it, although he did give Knox a quick once-over.

"Of course, sir," he said after a momentary pause. "Please come this way." He escorted Knox through the open doorway and down the corridor for a short distance, stopping at one of a row of seemingly identical doors.

Just as on the previous visit with Marianna a few hours back, Knox's escort held his smartphone to the doorknob and buzzed the door open. Only this time it opened, not on Nyquist's commodious corner office, but on a small windowless chamber sporting only a single straight-backed chair. No other amenities in sight—not even a pile of months-old magazines such as were to be found cluttering every level surface in the typical doctor's waiting room.

As he walked in, Knox took his own phone out, inadvertently bumping it into the one the orderly was just then pocketing.

"Sorry," he told the man.

"No problem, sir," that worthy replied. "If you'll just have a seat, I'll go see if Deputy Director Nyquist is available." He closed the door quietly behind him.

Knox sat there for a while drumming his fingers on his knee. When that got old, he rose and tried the knob.

Locked.

———

A good fifteen minutes went by, and Knox was still cooling his heels in the windowless, evidently escape-proof waiting room, with nothing to indicate that Nyquist's arrival was any more imminent than when the orderly had stashed him in here to begin with.

There was, however, *some*thing going on outside. Pressing his ear to the door, Knox could hear what sounded like a throng of people hustling down the corridor, talking amongst themselves. Too indistinct to pick up on what they were saying for the most part.

Then two voices came clear, passing just outside the door.

"So, what, you left him in there by himself, Liam?"

"What else was I supposed to do? The Doctor will be along after the gathering. Mr. Knox will keep till then."

"But ... it's the *Father!*"

"Think I don't know that? Look, he's not in any danger. He can't get past the locks. And even if he could, he'd never get through the ground-floor intrusion countermeasures. It's like I said: he'll keep."

The voices were fading into the distance. The last thing

Knox heard—or thought he heard—was, "I hope to the Old Ones you're right."

Knox strained an ear, but it had gone quiet again outside. Wherever that mob was headed, they were no longer in the immediate vicinity. He was alone once more in the so-called "waiting room" and free to ponder his options.

As to those options, well, he'd promised Marianna not to do anything she wouldn't do. Question was: What *would* she do in a spot like this?

More to the point, what could *he* do?

He twisted the doorknob, rattled it. Nothing. A locked-room mystery, for sure.

Fortunately, the solution was right there in his pocket. He'd made note of the use of the smartphone access pass on his earlier visit to SGI, this time he was ready. He took out his iPhone and backed up to the start of the NFC transmissions it had been capturing ever since he'd entered the building.

Near-Field Communications, NFC for short, was a wonderful technology, perfect for so-called contactless credit card payments and hands-free vehicle entry and ignition systems. And, of course, facility-access capabilities, such as the one Knox's orderly friend had used to unlock the door to his holding cell. Best of all, the signal itself only had an effective range of a few centimeters, making even an unencrypted NFC transmission devilishly hard to intercept.

Unless, of course, you somehow happened to be standing right next to the guy who was using NFC to unlock something, and, ideally, managed to accidentally bump up against the transmitting device, as Knox had done.

Holding his breath, Knox positioned his iPhone against the doorknob and pressed "Play" on its NFC capture.

And was rewarded with a resounding *buzz*.

Knox was past the lock, through the door, out into SGI's main corridor, and free at last. Maybe.

Only ...

Hadn't that Liam guy been saying something about "countermeasures"?

Knox felt it before he heard it. Could hardly hear it at all, in fact. At most, it was just a low, almost subsonic thrum. Whatever it was, it seemed to be coming from all around him, filling the ambient space to overflowing, setting his internal organs to vibrating in synch with it.

Vibration, that was the key. Somehow he was being immersed in an envelope of infrasound: low-frequency sound waves below the range of audibility, but not—unfortunately— entirely beyond the range of perception.

He whistled, impressed despite himself. Intrusion countermeasures, indeed! Subaudible infrasonics of the kind generated by wind turbines or earthquakes or even antiquated household plumbing had long been known to produce sensations of dizziness and dread in human subjects. There were even cases of heart failure triggered by too great a proximity to the mammoth stage subwoofers featured at rock concerts.

And there was one more effect: High-intensity infrasound was also capable of inducing vibrations in the eyeball and optic nerve—vibrations which could result in hallucinations.

That seemed to be what Knox was experiencing now. The lighting in the corridor had begun flickering, dimming and brightening, colors swirling faster and faster until he felt as though he were trapped inside a rapidly gyrating kaleidoscope. Between that and the low-frequency rumbles shaking his innards, it was all he could do to beat back the waves of nausea threatening to engulf him.

As he advanced down the corridor, the flat planes of the walls, ceiling, and floor seemed to buckle and bulge. Then they began shifting, sliding, folding into nightmarish origamis. And the angles at which the cross-corridors intersected the hall he was walking down kept rotating into the oblique or acute, anything but true.

He'd been here before: The whole experience was starting to feel like a flashback to that one bad trip back in grad school—the one that had come close to driving him over the edge into full-blown psychosis. Still, close only counts in horseshoes and hand grenades. *Get a grip,* he told himself. He'd survived that pharmacological dark night of the soul. He could make it through this mechanically induced version too.

Not that this time around was any more tolerable for being externally imposed. It was as if the geometry of the building was reconfiguring itself as he moved through it. He could hear voices and crowd noises echoing indistinctly off in the far distance, but no amount of walking seemed to bring them any nearer. Dizzy and disoriented, Knox stopped and stared at the now-empty front lobby he'd first come in by. Had he been walking in circles? How was he ever going to find Persephone in this labyrinth?

For lack of alternatives, Knox tried squeezing his eyes shut. Better. At least this way he wasn't being distracted by the delusory visuals. Eyes closed, hand grazing the wall for guidance, Knox did his best to ignore the palpitations of his heart and the somersaults in his stomach. He eased his way down the corridor toward the sound of the crowd voices he'd heard before. Only now they seemed to be getting marginally louder.

He nearly stumbled when his groping hand suddenly encountered a gap in the wall he'd been feeling his way along.

A stairwell of some sort. *That hadn't been there before, had it?* At least he hadn't seen it, and what did that prove?

Feeling around, he found a handrail. He probed gingerly with an outstretched foot and bumped into the first riser of a staircase leading to the upper reaches of the Institute. Fear of stumbling forced him to open his eyes, whereupon he was surprised to find that the stairs looked perfectly normal, with none of the distortions and contortions of the first-floor corridor he'd just left. The vague, seasick feeling that had been with him ever since he'd left the waiting room had begun subsiding too.

Clutching the handrail, he clambered up the steps as quick as he could, lest the mirages kick in again and leave him blind, sick, and stranded somewhere short of the top.

He let out a sigh of relief to find himself standing safe and sound on the solid, unshifting floor of the Institute's second story. He paused momentarily, recovering from the last vestiges of vertigo. Those were *some* "intrusion countermeasures"!

But why? What kind of intrusion were they expecting to have to counter? What Knox had experienced down below was enough to give a SWAT team pause.

Who in the hell *were* these people?

Knox had a feeling he was about to find out. From up here, the voices were definitely louder, if no more understandable. And they seemed to be coming from above, from the top of yet another flight of stairs.

Eyes wide open now, he followed the crowd noises up to the Institute's third floor.

Knox stood in a hidden alcove just inside a voluminous amphitheater of a room where the voices had been coming from until a moment ago. It was a vantage point with an unobstructed view of an arched double-height ceiling and a semicircle of what looked like pews arrayed beneath it. And, filling those pews, was a capacity crowd. Looked like the bulk of the SGI staff, just now quieting down in anticipation of...*what, exactly?*

In the center of that space, a giant plasma screen hung down above a pulpit-like affair. Blank when Knox had first entered, the display now showed the backlit outline of a man standing at a rostrum. A caption identified him as StarChild's Director, Dr. Dietrich Schaefer. Knox strained his eyes but could make out no more than a darkened silhouette.

The voice, too, when it came, sounded anonymized, lacking in intonation, almost synthetic.

"I want to thank you all," Schaefer began, "for coming together here in our Sanctuary on such short notice, taking precious time away from pressing duties here at the End of All Things. But I trust you will be happy to hear that our Deputy Director, Brother Nyquist, has gladsome tidings—truly momentous news—to share with us all. So without further ado, I will turn this meeting over to him. Brother?"

The crowd—or was it more a congregation?—looked up expectantly as Lars Nyquist made his way to the podium beneath the flatscreen. A few scattered shouts echoed off the rafters high above. Hard to make out what they were shouting about, though Knox caught what sounded like "Old Ones," maybe a few interspersed "Hosannahs."

"Behold!" As Nyquist uttered that word, an aperture irised open at the apex of the vault, and a single shaft of light shone down onto a raised platform in the middle of the auditorium.

There was something wrong with that light. It didn't look like natural sunlight or, for that matter, any kind of manmade illumination. There was something altogether unearthly about it. And that wasn't all....

For there, on the platform, her tiny body bathed in that eldritch luminosity, lay...Persephone.

"Behold," Nyquist thundered. "The Child is with us! Safe and secure at last, here in our Sanctuary!"

As if the Deputy Director had thrown a switch, pandemonium broke loose. Cries of "Praise be to the Old Ones!" reverberated throughout the vast open space. Lab coats and civilian garments were rent. Two women and an elderly man fainted dead away and lay there on the floor unmoving and unheeded by the rest of the congregants.

Knox could hardly believe what he was seeing. Whatever this was, it was no kind of treatment, not by any stretch of the imagination. He was getting a sinking feeling that he'd delivered his daughter into the hands of, not a team of geneticists, but some sort of diabolical cabal.

As if he'd read Knox's mind, the Deputy Director was now saying, "Ignorant outsiders would brand StarChild a cult. And what of it? The Pythagoreans of ancient Greece too were called a cult in their time, yet they bequeathed to the world magnificent theorems of order and elegance and a sacred oath still sworn by physicians down to the present day, though mistakenly attributed to Hippocrates. But StarChild can do more than that ..."

And with that as prelude, Nyquist began leading his followers through a catechism of sorts.

"Yes, we can do much more than that," he repeated. "We can impart, to any with the wit and the will to listen, the truth of human history.

"A history about to come to an end.

"For the Emissary has at last begun the Transfiguration." Nyquist's voice rang out over the multitude.

"Praise be to the Old Ones," the congregation chanted in unison.

"The Final Hour of Halfway Humanity is at hand," he intoned.

"Praise be to the Old Ones," they chorused again.

"Halfway Humanity?" That sounded oddly familiar to Knox. Something Mycroft had mentioned back when he was researching SGI, perhaps?

But Nyquist was still haranguing the crowd. "Raise up the Child!" he shouted.

The assembled multitude surged toward the sunlit dais where Persephone lay sleeping.

That did it for Knox. Leaving the seclusion of the entryway, he forced his way through the assembled worshippers, heedless of the shouts rising in his wake. Before he could reach the dais, though, he found himself bear-hugged, body locked, and slammed to the hardwood floor by two beefy uniformed security-guard types.

"Be careful not to hurt him," the Deputy Director shouted from the podium. "Just escort him to my office. And gently—it's the Father!"

1700 HOURS: BOILERPLATE

Never in his life had Knox been manhandled more politely than on this frogmarch from the Institute's topmost story down to Nyquist's ground-floor office. Apparently, being "the Father" counted for something here at SGI. The kid-gloves treatment had its limits, though. In particular, his accompanying brace of security goons saw no need to relax their bone-crushing grip on his arms.

Thankfully, the *trompe l'oeil* effects that had hampered Knox's earlier trek through the first-floor hallway were nowhere in evidence on the return trip. At the end, he was back in the office where he and Marianna had met with Nyquist a scant three hours ago.

Having installed Knox in one of the visitor chairs, his escort turned around and made to leave. The lead goon paused just long enough to announce, "The Deputy Director will be in to see you shortly." He then exited, locking the door behind him.

Promises, promises. It was a full quarter hour—hardly Knox's idea of "shortly"—before Nyquist himself entered the room, seated himself at his desk, and favored his visitor with a penetrating stare.

"Well, Mr. Knox," he said finally. "I'm sure you must have questions."

"You bet your ass I do, Doctor. Or should I say 'Brother'? Starting with *what the hell was that all about?*"

"You're referring, no doubt, to our little gathering just now." Nyquist sighed. "All in the name of maintaining the allegiance and enthusiasm of our followers."

"So this was—what?—a fundraising rally?"

"Not at all. The Institute has other, far more munificent sources of revenue to draw on, let me assure you. No, our adherents are merely needed to serve as foot soldiers, firmly committed to the cause, should any—shall we say—unforeseen eventualities arise."

"So cannon fodder, then."

"What of it? It's not as if our poor, deluded followers wouldn't have latched on to some other belief system, had Star-Child not indoctrinated them first. No, the matrix from which a cult arises is what social psychologists dub the 'cultic milieu.' It's more like a culture in a Petri dish than any kind of rational social movement: a seething medium ready to incubate any new viral meme and nurture it into hothouse growth. At least what we are feeding them has the virtue of being *true*. We aren't conning our faithful, so much as providing them—in their eagerness to believe in *any*thing—with something *real* to believe in."

"Something 'real' involving my daughter?"

"Please believe me, Mr. Knox, I can understand how difficult all this must be for you."

"Well, it's about to get a good deal more difficult—for *you*, Nyquist! I've come to take Persephone out of this madhouse and, given what I've just seen, to consider following up with legal action."

Nyquist leaned back in his chair. "I'm very much afraid none of that will be possible, Mr. Knox. As you will see if you will be so good as to check the release form that you and Ms. Knox both signed upon Persephone's admission ..."

"Release form? You mean that stack of boilerplate you shoved in front of us?"

"That boilerplate, as you call it, gives SGI the right—more, the obligation—to pursue any course of treatment we deem to be in the best interest of the patient. Under the circumstances ..."

"Does that 'treatment' include the right to feature Persephone as the centerpiece of some sort of satanic ritual?"

"It is unfortunate that you had to witness our, uh, welcoming ceremony. But that is neither here nor there as far as the Child's welfare is concerned."

Once again, Knox could hear the capitalization when Nyquist said the word "Child."

"Welcoming ceremony, hell! This is bullshit. We demand to have Persephone released into our care immediately!"

"I'm afraid I cannot authorize that. It could be life-threatening, given that the Child's treatment is at a critical stage."

"But you're *not* treating her. That's the point. If necessary, I'll go to the authorities and get a warrant for her discharge."

"I'm afraid you will find that also rather difficult to do. The Institute's lawyers, most of whom are themselves members of the StarChild congregation, are prepared to seek an injunction against any such action. In addition, I think you will find that these so-called authorities, whose recent campaigns the Institute has supported more than generously, will be predisposed to rule in our favor. And particularly so, when it comes down to a case of a distraught but uninformed parent's opinion versus that of medical experts."

For once, Knox had no reply. He just sat there stunned.

"And now, if you'll excuse me, Mr. Knox, there is not much time left—not for any of us, I'm afraid—and I am, as you can see, a very busy man."

So saying, Nyquist pressed a call button on his desk phone. Security must have been waiting right outside the office, because they entered immediately and—less gently than on the way in—escorted Knox to SGI's University Place exit.

Knox trudged back through Washington Square Park, through scattered flakes of snow, fuming.

He'd been effectively denied access to Persephone. To the Institute as a whole, probably, given the way he and Nyquist had parted company—though he'd yet to verify that.

It was, he felt, almost as though Persephone had been kidnapped. By her own doctors, no less.

Knox had had to investigate a kidnapping once before—just this past February, in fact—although nothing to compare with this situation in regards to its personal aspects, of course.

And that hadn't been a real kidnapping anyway. That is, it had been real, but it was an abduction intended to safeguard the abductee. It had been masterminded by a very strange abductor indeed: the artificial general intelligence that called itself—or, give the devil his due, *who* called *him*self—Nietzsche.

That stray thought spurred Knox to once again briefly consider reaching out to the AI for help. For a moment, he found himself tempted to break his strict "just say no to machine superintelligence" rule. But then, there was no telling how the superintelligence in question might react in this sort of situation. Despite their having worked together cheek by virtual jowl for days on end, most of the time Nietzsche's motivations and thought processes—his very psychology—had remained utterly opaque to Knox, bearing only the scantest resemblance to anything human.

After all, hadn't Nietzsche famously tried to protect the one human being he undeniably cared about—Fatimah Ansari, the seven-year-old heiress he referred to (metaphorically, of course) as his "sister"—by the problematical device of hiring a gang of ex-KGB thugs to spirit her away?

Add to that gaping character flaw, the fact that Nietzsche was a "person" of interest in several ongoing federal investigations. Not to mention that he gave Knox the unsettling, but hardly unjustified feeling of being *watched* all the time, and ...

No, all things considered, he wasn't even going to go there.

All things considered, Freddy had nowhere else to go.

Over the past eight hours, Nietzsche's semi-autonomous Pairidaeza instantiation had been working with the on-site medical staff and state-of-the-art facilities, trying to reverse or even just arrest the worsening of Fatimah's condition.

All to no avail. The little girl's temperature was now one hundred and two degrees Fahrenheit and still climbing, albeit slowly. Thankfully she appeared to be experiencing no pain. On the other hand, she had fallen into a deep, almost comatose slumber from which no external stimulus seemed able to rouse her.

Loathe as he was to interfere with the principal AI reification's important work, Freddy also knew—it being the very reason for his quasi-independent existence, after all—that Nietzsche would want to be apprised immediately of any threats to Fatimah's health and well-being. And, much as Freddy might have wished it otherwise, that's what the current situation was shaping up to be—a threat.

There truly was no other option than to appeal to the main Nietzsche persona residing in the WellGrid satellite network orbiting two-hundred-fifty miles overhead.

Having reluctantly arrived at this conclusion, Freddy set about establishing contact. And ...

Strange! Freddy couldn't recall a time when such an attempt at communication had failed. He reviewed the status of the link terminus here at the Pairidaeza end, only to find all the readings coming back in the green. He ratcheted up the message's priority and tried sending it again, with no more success than the first time around.

Either the comm link was down, or Nietzsche himself had gone incommunicado for reasons which could only be guessed at.

Either way, Freddy was on his own.

Marianna looked up as Jon entered their hotel room, stamping residual slush off his shoes. One look at his face, and she could tell something was very, very wrong.

"Jon, what's the matter?"

"It was a mistake to put Persephone in the care of that so-called Institute," he said miserably. "And I'm not sure how to rectify it."

"Slow down, Jon. One thing at a time: What mistake are you talking about?"

As if his legs would no longer support him, Jon slumped into an armchair opposite her bed. He cradled his head in his hands. "StarChild is not what it seems. Not at all."

Marianna knew that tone, though she'd rarely heard it—Jon was on the verge of giving up. Rather than permit herself to succumb to the panic she could feel building inside her, Marianna deliberately shifted into impersonal interrogation mode. "Let me get this straight: it's *not* a genetics lab?"

"That part's just a front, far as I can tell. If anything, Star-Child is more like a religious sect."

"What makes you say that?"

"I wish you could have been with me when I was over there

just now. I blundered into what I can only describe as some sort of cultic ritual, complete with Lars Nyquist leading a flock of true believers in some sort of whacked-out catechism, featuring —if you can believe it—our daughter as the star attraction."

"*What?*" Marianna abandoned any attempt at keeping her professional cool.

"I only wish I'd thought to snap a picture or two before I tried to interfere. But, yeah. There she was, lying on a pedestal, bathed in some sort of weird light. And with all these people around her chanting 'Praise be to the Old Ones,' or something to that effect."

"And there was no sign they were attempting to cure her?"

Jon shook his head. "What I saw looked more like Heaven's Gate than Memorial Sloan Kettering."

"Jon, we've got to get Persephone out of there!"

"You think I didn't try? I went to grab her and head for the exit, only to get collared by SGI Security. I thought for sure they were going to beat the crap out of me, but apparently I get some sort of special dispensation, on account of being 'the Father' in this little Holy Family Christmas pageant thing they've got going on. In the end, all the gendarmes did—very politely, mind you—was hustle me off to see Nyquist himself."

"What did Dr. Nyquist have to say?"

"It was all very civilized, on his part at least. But he wouldn't hear of discharging Persephone from the Institute. *And* he claimed they had the law on their side, and that we'd waived our right to interfere in Persephone's treatment when we signed those admittance forms."

"There must be *some*one we can go to."

"That was the other thing. Nyquist as much as admitted that they've got the authorities in their pocket. That he was going to see to it that any appeal to child welfare or anyone else was going to wind up buried beneath a mountain of paperwork so deep it'd never see the light of day."

"Can they even do that?"

"Not forever," Jon said, "but maybe long enough."

Marianna didn't have to ask what he meant by that. A long enough delay, and it wouldn't matter anymore.

Persephone would be dead.

1800 HOURS: NUCLEAR OPTION

Lars Nyquist sat alone at his desk, mulling the just-ended meeting with Jonathan Knox. Or not quite alone: Dietrich Schaefer was with him, virtually if not in person.

"How did it go?" the Director asked.

"You were listening in, were you not?"

"Always. I was merely inquiring as to your perspective."

"Ah. Well, from my perspective, I think I've succeeded in buying us the time we need."

"You may have bought us less time than you appear to think."

"What makes you say that?"

"Have you looked into Marianna Bonaventure's professional background or associations at all?"

The day's events were all coming at Marianna harder and faster than she could handle. First, the bottomless pit of despair that had yawned open at her feet on being told her baby, her newborn, was dying. Followed almost immediately by a rush of relief bordering on euphoria with word of StarChild Genomics's purported miracle cure. And now, just as suddenly, that hope had been dashed utterly, SGI's veneer of expertise stripped away to reveal—what had Jon called it?—some sort of cult lurking in the shadows behind the facade?

She took a deep breath. Couldn't give in to this. Not now, not while there was still a chance they could at least get their baby back. Not until they had explored all the avenues still open to them. Beginning with the most obvious one.

"How do we know this Dr. Nyquist wasn't just bluffing?" she asked.

Jon raised his head. "Bluffing about what?"

"That business about how the powers that be were under the Institute's thumb. I mean, we're Persephone's parents, aren't we? That's got to count for something."

"I'm sure it would," Jon said, "but only at the tag end of a long, long trail of litigation. I *don't* think Nyquist was bluffing about the amount of legal firepower they're prepared to bring to bear. *Pro bono* too, given that they've apparently got any number of lawyers among their true believers."

"So what does that leave us with? How about the police?"

He sighed. "Let me give it a try."

Marianna listened while Jon called in, had his call transferred through a number of intermediaries, and finally wound up in conversation with someone for about fifteen minutes. He wasn't doing much of the talking, though, save for the intermittent "Yeses" and "Nos" and, once or twice, protestations of "You just don't understand!"

At the end of all that, Jon rang off with a final, "Right, then. You'll be hearing from our lawyers." For a moment there, it looked as if he were going to hurl the phone against the wall, but he settled for shoving it back in his shirt pocket and muttering, "Damn!"

"What was that all about?" Marianna asked.

Jon shook his head. "Outmaneuvered again. StarChild has filed a preemptive complaint against *me*, for God's sakes. Claimed I disrupted a religious service, violated their First Amendment rights. They're willing to drop charges, but only if we do the same."

Marianna bit her lip. "Jon, isn't there anything we can do?"

"Not us. You," he said. "I think the time has come for you to have a conversation with your boss."

"What about?" she asked. But she was afraid she already knew the answer.

"What else? The nuclear option."

Knox waited for Marianna to respond. To say something—anything. When she finally did, it was nothing he wanted to hear.

"Don't think I wouldn't like to, Jon," she said. "God knows, from what you've told me, if anyone deserves to be on the receiving end of a reconnaissance in force, it's this StarChild outfit."

"But...?"

Marianna expelled a breath. "It's just, I don't think there's a chance in hell of getting CROM to come in on this."

"Why not?" Knox asked, trying with marginal success to keep the desperation out of his voice. The US Department of Energy's Critical Resources Oversight Mandate was their ace in the hole, dammit! It was the only resource they had left to call on. They couldn't just give up on it.

"Think about it from Pete's point of view." Marianna didn't look any happier about what she was saying than he was hearing it. "You're talking about a full-scale paramilitary exercise, in the middle of downtown Manhattan, no less. Forget about the potential risk to life and limb. The cost alone would be prohibitive. No way Pete'd go for it."

But the words "paramilitary exercise" had triggered a memory.

"What if it weren't?" Knox said slowly. "Prohibitive, that is?"

"What do you mean? Do you have any notion of what it'd cost to organize an op like this on such short notice?"

Knox held up a hand. "I didn't mention this before, because it didn't seem relevant, but when I was down at Federal Plaza a few hours back, the place was kind of chaotic. Major refits going on in preparation for some sort of weekend wargame, Jack told me."

"Oh, right." It was coming back to Marianna now. "CROM's so-called 'Christmas Party.' It's a big MOUT—that's Military Operations on Urban Terrain, Jon—joint exercise that Compliance stages with Interdiction every year around this time.

"But what's that got to do with ... Oh!"

Marianna breathed a sigh of relief. It had taken a while, but Jon had finally agreed to leave the negotiations with CROM to her. Jon's own history with the Mandate was fraught, to put it mildly. And that went double for her husband's relationship with Marianna's boss, head of CROM's Reacquisition Directorate, Euripides "Pete" Aristos, in particular.

Jon and Pete had been butting heads basically from the get-go. Of course, it didn't help matters that, on their very first encounter, Jon had managed to hijack her boss's air-gapped desktop computer—with her boss sitting right there at the keyboard. And then again, just this year in fact, there was the infamous Valentine's Day incident, where Pete had had Jon marked for termination by CROM's in-house Interdiction task force—although that was all just a misunderstanding, really.

Trouble was, lately Jon seemed to be under the mistaken impression that her marrying him had buried the hatchet once and for all. And so far Marianna hadn't had the opportunity, or the heart, to disabuse him.

Marianna, on the other hand, was the closest thing to a daughter her crusty old lifelong bachelor of a boss had ever had. No question: as far as Pete and all of CROM were concerned, she really *was* family. And, by extension, her child should be as well.

Time to put that last assumption to the test. Having secured Jon's promise to listen in, but not speak a word, she keyed in Pete's direct number.

Pete picked up on the second ring. "Marianna? Congratulations! A girl, isn't it? What name did you decide on?"

She got as far as "Hi, Pete" before she began sobbing.

"Marianna, what's wrong?"

She couldn't recall ever having heard Pete sounding so ... so concerned before.

"It's complicated, Pete. Our baby... Persephone is her name, thanks for asking. Our baby is sick. Really sick. So sick, she may even die."

"God, no! What is it?"

"Some sort of weird genetic malfunction. Triploidy, it's called. Except it's not like any case of triploidy anyone's ever seen. It has her doctors baffled. That's about the only thing giving us any hope at all."

"So there *is* hope, then?"

"There was, until... Actually, that's what I'm calling about, Pete."

"Tell me."

Somehow, Marianna got through the whole story with an absolute minimum of muffled weeping. Describing how the team at Saint Bart's seemed to have stumbled on a treatment of sorts. But then how she and Jon had transferred Persephone to a biotech startup, StarChild Genomics, lured by what turned out to be false promises of a cure. And how StarChild was now flat-out refusing to release the infant.

"Can they even do that?" Pete broke in. "Hold on to her against the parents' wishes, I mean?"

"They're maintaining that they can. That we signed away our right to second-guess StarChild's treatment protocols once we had Persephone admitted. But they're *not* treating her, is the point. They've got some kind of bizarre cult-worship thing going on instead."

"Can't you get a court order, then?"

"Not in time to do any good. StarChild's Deputy Director has already warned us they're going to lawyer up and fight any action we bring against them. And forget about going to the police. We tried."

Marianna hesitated a moment, then made her big ask: "It's why I'm talking to *you*, Pete. To see if there isn't something CROM can do."

Pete was silent for a long moment. Then he said, "You've got a STU-5 simulator installed on your computer, right?"

"Uh-huh." STU-5 was short for Secure Terminal Unit V. And actually, the simulator was installed not on her laptop, but on Jon's. Still, no reason to share *that* detail with her boss. It would only tick him off.

"Okay, then. I'm going to ring off. Later."

"Later," of course, meant momentarily. Jon already had the STU up and running by the time Pete linked back in, this time with full video of her boss's face, frown and all.

"That's better," he said. "Now, just for the record—or, actually, *off* the record—you and I never had this conversation. So what do you need?"

Marianna didn't mince words. "Brute force," she said.

"Enough shock and awe to effect a contested entry *cum* search-and-rescue on Institute premises."

Pete gave out a low whistle. "I thought that's where you might be headed."

"Well, is it doable or not?"

"I can't see how, Marianna. Believe me, I wish I could."

"But, but what about the CROM Christmas Party? Couldn't you somehow just move that MOUT exercise up a couple days?"

"And crosstown into the bargain? That much of a reconfig would raise all sorts of questions, what with the year-end audit right around the corner. And my fingerprints would be all over it."

As much as his words themselves, Pete's expression told Marianna this wasn't going to fly. What had she been thinking? Divert an entire training exercise on behalf of one tiny infant, who was—a momentary pause here while she forced herself to confront the unthinkable—who was likely to die in any case? No way.

But there was still one thing that might work. She'd held off mentioning it till now for fear her boss wouldn't believe it. Hell, she wasn't sure she believed it herself, but her back was to the wall. What did she have to lose?

"Listen up, Pete, it's not just our baby—there's something that just feels wrong about this whole StarChild setup.... You know Jack Adler, right?"

"The black-hole guy?"

"Right, well..." *Here goes,* "Jack seems to think StarChild Genomics has been snagging unidentified signals ... from outer space."

"Not aliens again." Pete groaned. "Won't we ever live down that *X-Files* malarkey?"

"Pete, I'm serious. Or Jack is, anyway. He says NASA's Planetary Protection Office put him on to it. You can check it out with him. He's down at the New York office as we speak."

Pete fell silent, leaving Marianna to hope against hope that he was still thinking it over, still trying to come up with a way to make this last-ditch scheme work.

But, when he did break his silence, what he came back with was, "Sorry, girl, this is way above my pay grade. Without NSC-level authorization, it'd be more than my job's worth. Yours too, for that matter."

Marianna had no reply to that, just sat there, tears running down her face.

For his part, Pete was sitting there silently, one hand massaging his balding pate. Marianna had seen him do that before, when he was turning some no-win decision over in his head.

"What the hell!" he burst out suddenly. "Look, there's one more thing I can try. I'm going offline now to check it out."

"What about me, Pete? What am I supposed to do?"

"You? You just hang tight. And, whatever you do, don't let this line drop!"

The Secure Terminal simulator reverted to its rest state.

Marianna waited as the minutes passed. Three became five. Then ten. Fifteen.

At the eighteen-minute mark, the STU-V window on Jon's laptop lit up again. A youngish face with a largish nose and a receding hairline stared out of it. Marianna returned the stare, but it was no one she knew.

He evidently knew her, though. "Ms. Bonaventure?" he said, pressing a button, "Please hold for the SecDef."

"Actually, it's Mrs. Knox now..." Marianna began. Then her mind caught up with the rest of the words.

Jesus Christ! Had Pete gone to the freaking Secretary of Defense?

Sure enough, the STU-V was now displaying the DoD seal: an eagle, wings spread beneath an arc of thirteen stars, talons grasping a clutch of arrows. Then that image too dissolved to reveal a hard-bitten, old-line New England face—framed by iron-gray curls and wearing an altogether uncharacteristic smile.

"Marianna!" Helen Artemis Gallagher exclaimed. "So good to see you again, dear. It's been too long."

It had, in fact, been only a little over ten months since Marianna had gone tracking the SecDef through the labyrinthine corridors of the Pairidaeza estate. She'd arrived just in time to prevent Gallagher's assassination at the hands of the terrorist mastermind Hamza al-Ahwazi.

It was an introduction Marianna had never forgotten. Nor, judging by the warm welcome, had Helen Gallagher.

"It's good to see you again too, Madame Sec—"

"Please, Marianna." Gallagher cut her off. "Just Helen. 'Madame Secretary' is for people who *haven't* saved my life."

"Thank you, Helen," Marianna mumbled.

"Better. Now, what can I do for you? Pete Aristos tells me you could use some help."

To Marianna's surprise, this time she got all the way through her story without a single sob. If anything, it was Gallagher who seemed on the brink of tears.

If so, she recovered her equanimity in record time. "Well, I'm sure you realize," she said briskly, "that personal considerations can in no way influence an operational decision of this magnitude."

Marianna nodded numbly. She should have expected no more. What was that old Russian saying Jon liked to quote? "Druzhba druzhba, a sluzhba sluzhba.". *Friendship is friendship, but duty is duty*. About summed it up.

But Gallagher wasn't done talking. "This NASA intercept, on the other hand ... I checked with my folks over at No Such Agency. Turns out NSA's been tracking the same signal, from the same source. And it's two-way."

"So it's really real, then?"

"Real enough to get the brass pissing their pants. Meaning, real enough for me to authorize a tactical infiltration of this StarChild facility ASAP."

Yes! Marianna felt dizzy with relief. She reached out to grasp Jon's hand, squeeze it hard.

Pete, God bless him, had gone and found someone for whom this all was definitely *not* above their paygrade.

"Pete Aristos'll take point, " Gallagher was going on, "seeing as he's already got the resources committed and ready to deploy. Rasmussen over at Energy's already okayed an inter-agency op."

Then, no longer bothering to hide her grin, the Secretary of Defense added, "'Course, if the strike force should just happen to come across this baby of yours in the process, well ..."

PART 3

———

RAID

EVENING, LAST DAY OF AUTUMN

1900 HOURS: LOGISTICS

Pete got back to her on the STU within the hour, looking more harried than Marianna had ever seen him.

"How goes it, Pete?" she asked.

"It's goes," her boss replied. "I've got a Chinook helo standing by at Bolling Air Force Base. Liftoff's in about an hour. If I pull out all the stops, we can chopper the full Christmas Party complement—that's ten Compliance and thirty Interdiction headcount—up from DC with an ETA about two and a half hours from now, but—"

"But what?"

"It's Manhattan, for Chrissake, Marianna. There's only a couple viable landing zone options on the whole damned island. And trucking the team over from either LZ to the target site will take a good half hour all by itself."

"Um, which landing zones were you looking at?"

"Well, there's the Wall Street heliport down at the southern tip of Manhattan, and West 30th Street over on the Hudson. Whichever way you slice it, you're looking at another, say, twenty-five to thirty minutes travel time through downtown traffic. Then we've got battlespace reconnaissance to consider, and tactical coordination. Lots of moving parts."

Marianna took a breath to object, but Pete was still rattling on. "That's another thing. Have we even got any intel on the layout of the target facility?"

Marianna shot a look at Jon. He gave her a tentative thumbs-up. It would have to do.

"Yes, to that. We've had someone scout it out." Out of the corner of her eye, Marianna saw Jon miming for her to mute the call.

"Wait one, Pete," she said, then hit the mute button and turned to her husband. "Yes, Jon, what is it?"

"About that target facility, they should be aware it's not going to be a walk in the park. Nyquist boasted about the Institute being able to field a force of what he called 'foot soldiers.' Judging from the size of the crowd at his 'prayer gathering,' that could be anywhere from fifty to a hundred guys."

Marianna absorbed this, nodded. "Put me back on the STU please, Jon."

"And one other thing," Jon began.

She swiped a hand to cut him off. "Not now. Pete's got too much on his plate as it is. Just unmute the STU for me."

Then: "Pete? Just a heads-up: There's good reason to believe StarChild could mount some kind of resistance. Best be loaded for bear."

"I'm going to assume you meant non-lethal bear." Pete was referencing CROM doctrine for operations on urban terrain: no use of deadly force where civilians might inadvertently stray into the line of fire.

"By the book. Roger that."

"Yeah, about that: If we *were* going by the book, the planning phase alone on an op like this would take a couple of days. We're trying to stand this whole thing up by the time the theaters let out tonight."

"I know, Pete. Believe me, I know. And don't think I don't appreciate it. What's your best guesstimate?"

"Figure four or five hours total. Say kickoff at midnight, just to be on the safe side."

Midnight! What could have happened to Persephone by then?

What couldn't?

"That's not going to cut it, Pete. Any chance we could shave off an hour or two at the least?"

"Tell me how."

"Um, let me think ... How about if we forget the heliports? Have the Chinook touch down in Washington Square Park instead. That's only half a block from the target. Saves us a half hour right there."

A moment while Pete scrolled the sat-view up to Greenwich Village. "Too many trees," he said when he got there. "Park benches, lampposts, your occasional late-night dog-walker, you name it."

"What if they land in the fountain basin?" Marianna countered. "That's a big, flat, circular area, almost like a helipad. The fountain itself doesn't stick out more than a foot above ground level, and it won't be running this time of year anyway. Bit of a tight squeeze, but hey, that's what they get paid the big bucks for, right?"

Pete didn't dignify that with a reply, just grunted.

"Please, Pete. It's my baby."

"Sounds like a plan," was all he said.

Knox waited while Marianna said her goodbyes to Aristos.

"Whew!" She smiled. "Whoever said paramilitary ops are like baseball had it right on the money: Long hours of tedium, brief moments of panic. Ah well, at least we've got a handle on the lay of the land."

"Um, yeah, about that," Knox started.

"Why? What's wrong?"

"The lay of the land," he said. "That was the other thing I didn't get a chance to go over with you. That building layout is way more complicated than you'd think."

"How complicated could it be? You've been there. For that matter, *I've* been there. Enough to know the basic floor plan, anyway."

"That's just it," Knox said. "When I went back the second time, things had all changed around. It was like walking through a hall of funhouse mirrors, minus the fun."

"What do you mean?"

Knox swallowed hard, reliving the experience. "It was like there were no right angles to anything, and the walls kept shifting around totally at random. As if I were stuck inside a house of cards that kept collapsing, reshuffling, restructuring itself with every step I took. At the same time there was this low-pitched, teeth-rattling vibration coming from everywhere. The overall effect had me totally weirded out—to the point where I thought I was going to upchuck."

"You're saying SGI has some sort of antipersonnel defenses in place. Kind of like that 'Havana syndrome' that was messing with our embassy staff in Cuba?"

He nodded. "'Intrusion countermeasures' is what I over-heard somebody call it. At the time I thought intrusion was a strange thing for SGI to be worrying about. Guess not. Anyway, the bottom line is: I'm afraid if we send a team into the Institute unprepared, they could wind up hopelessly disori-ented. Easy pickings for whatever ragtag militia Nyquist has managed to pull together."

"Assuming the same thing starts happening again, that is. But what do we do about it?"

Knox put his head down, swallowed again. "I think maybe I've got to go in there with them."

―――――

Marianna couldn't believe she was hearing this.

"Jon, don't take this the wrong way," she said, "but *are you out of your freaking mind?*"

"Why? What do you mean?"

"Just that it seems to me I remember a time, not so very long ago, when Interdiction had you in their crosshairs." They would have got him, too, if a mutual enemy hadn't beaten them to the punch. "And now...what? You're all going to join hands and sing 'Kum Ba Yah'?"

"Things have changed," he said under his breath.

"Not as much as you seem to think. Anyway, what could you possibly hope to accomplish?"

"At the very least I can hope to keep the team from blindly walking into an ambush."

"Jon, face facts: You've got no training, no skills. I mean, yes, you've got skills, plenty of 'em, but nothing applicable to this kind of situation."

Jon shrugged. "Granted. But, against all of those deficits, there's one thing I *do* have going for me."

"That being?"

"Motivation," he said. "She's my baby too."

Marianna had no ready answer for that, at least not while she was struggling to hold back a sudden rush of tears.

Finally, she managed to draw a breath. "Just keep your head down, okay?"

Then she held out her arms to him. As they embraced, she whispered in his ear, "I love you, you damned fool."

2000 HOURS: HORS DE COMBAT

After her husband had left for Federal Plaza to prep for the raid, Marianna was all alone once again, sitting up in bed in their hotel room. Sitting on her hands, more like.

Feeling useless.

But what else could she do? What with everything her body had been through over the past twenty-four hours, it was an effort just to make the round trip to the bathroom under her own power.

She paused and thought about that some more: *Under her own power* ... That was the operative phrase.

She hobbled over to the armchair, opened Jon's laptop and launched the Secure Terminal simulator one more time.

"'Sup, Marianna?"

She had to strain to make out the words. Pete's voice, usually so loud and clear—especially loud—was being nearly drowned out by the roar of heavy engines.

"Kind of busy here," he shouted, "in case you hadn't noticed."

"Hi, Pete. Just checking in to see how things are going," she lied.

"About as well as could be expected for a half-assed op like this. Takeoff's in fifteen. ETA around, um, 2130. Slight change of plan, though: we're making a pit stop at West 30th after all."

"What? Why's that?"

"Blame it on the intel you yourself supplied. If SGI's ready to put up a fight, there's no point in us sitting on the ground at their doorstep while we do our final run-throughs. Better if we get all that out of the way at an intermediate LZ, then load up again and barrel on in to Washington Square at the last minute. Element of surprise, 'case you hadn't heard of it."

Marianna could have done without the sarcasm, but she nodded. "Makes sense, I guess."

"Sorry you couldn't be with us," Pete added. "We really could've used you."

And that right there gave her just the opening she'd been hoping for.

"Hold that thought, Pete ..." And with no more preamble than that, she launched into her second, even bigger ask of the evening.

To his credit, Pete heard her out—for all of half a minute. Then he cut her off, coincidentally echoing almost word for word the objection she'd voiced to Jon not ten minutes ago.

"*Are you out of your fucking mind?*" Except that Pete followed it up with an, "*Absolutely not!*"

Nothing daunted, Marianna dug her heels in and began the protracted process of talking her boss around to a "yes."

For the second time that day, Knox took the ten-minute cab ride down to 26 Federal Plaza and checked in at CROM headquarters. The only difference was, this time they were waiting for him on the far side of the entryway's security scanner.

"Welcome to Critical Resources, Mr. Knox," said a young black woman whose nameplate identified her as Callista Bannister. "I understand you're going to be our native guide for the evening?"

Something in the way she'd phrased that question was enough to prompt a second look. A cap of tight brown curls, large brown eyes, mahogany complexion and...body armor?

"Uh, you're part of the SGI op, Ms. Bannister?"

"Yessir, second-in-command for the Christmas Party. Oh, and that's Captain Bannister, USMC, on loan to CROM Interdiction. Or you can call me Callie."

"Call me Jon." Knox held out his hand. "Pleasure to meet you, Callie."

They shook. "Likewise, Jon," she said, then turned and pointed him toward a locker. "C'mon, let's get you suited up."

2100 HOURS: SURPRISE PACKAGES

At the first sound of a knock, Marianna eased herself out of bed, and stood there shakily. She eyed the distance from the bedside to the hotel room door, thought better of it.

"Come on in, it's open," she shouted instead.

A ramrod-straight, crewcut type worked his way inside, maneuvering a hand truck through the entrance. What made the maneuvering ticklish was the truck's cargo: a massive wooden crate bearing the labels "This Side Up" and "MX-101a."

Christmas come early!

"Where would you like it, Deputy Director?"

Marianna was amused that the CROM functionary in charge of the delivery was doing his level best to observe the requisite formalities, even though he probably hadn't ever encountered a Deputy Director of CROM Reacquisitions attired in a nightgown and a small cup–size nursing bra before.

"Just set it right there in the corner. Oh, and please unpack it, if you wouldn't mind."

That latter operation took a good fifteen minutes, and a crowbar that the CROM guy had thoughtfully brought along for the trip. But when it was done, a gleaming metal contraption loomed in the indicated space: MX-101a, ready to rock 'n roll.

"And here's a little light reading." CROM guy grinned, handing her a softcover instruction manual with all the thickness and heft of one of those vintage Manhattan telephone directories. A sense of humor, then, despite appearances to the contrary.

She smiled back.

"Anything else, Deputy Director?" he asked.

"No, thank you..." she glanced at his nametag, "...uh, Brad. That'll be all. Much obliged."

Once Brad had stacked the packaging debris on the hand truck and wheeled it out into the corridor and away, Marianna walked over to the armchair and sat down to admire her "Christmas present." Now all she had to do was figure out how to operate the bloody thing.

She began paging through the manual, searching for the quick start guide. Ah, there it was, right up front. Who'd have guessed?

Humming to herself, Marianna began, in the few hours left to her, the job of mastering the nuts-and-bolts intricacies of the MX-101a. Too bad Jon had gone off to meet up with the CROM taskforce; she really could have used his help translating some of the technicalese.

On second thought, no—there was no way in hell she was going to try getting her husband on board with what she had planned for this supersized stocking stuffer.

Jonathan Knox stood on the tarmac at the West 30th Street heliport. A short distance away, the local CROM Compliance contingent clustered, awaiting reinforcements from DC—reinforcements flying in aboard the CH47-Chinook twin-rotor helo whose running lights were just now becoming visible through the night mist rising off the Hudson.

Knox glanced down at the body armor now encasing him. This SAM2X5-630 stuff it was fashioned from was a freaking marvel. With a thickness of two credit cards glued together, it had double the strength of tungsten carbide and could withstand a bullet impact from an M4 assault rifle without deforming. The secret was a process called spark plasma sintering. It used heat (630 degrees Celsius of it), pressure (1,300 atmospheres), and current (a hundred thousand amperes). The combination created crystalline structures within the metal. The end result was a material so strong that it was even being used to plate near-Earth satellites for protection against micrometeorite strikes.

Yeah, a marvel for sure. The only problem being that the damned armor made it virtually impossible to scratch the ferocious itch that was developing between his shoulder blades. He tried taking his mind off that by focusing instead on the Chinook as it vectored in for its landing.

The ramp at the rear of the helo dropped down, looking for all the world like the gaping mouth of a goliath grouper—for Knox's money, one of the ugliest fish in the sea. It looked good on the Chinook, though: easy egress for the full complement of thirty Interdiction agents plus a dozen Compliance guys now scrambling down the incline and assembling on the tarmac. The added firepower was a sight for sore eyes.

Less of a sight for sore eyes was the last man coming down the ramp. The last man Knox had been expecting to see here, in point of fact: CROM Reacquisitions Director Euripides "Pete" Aristos.

Aristos eyed the home-team reception party, looking vaguely surprised and not at all pleased to see Knox standing there among them.

"You!" was all he said, but he managed to pack a boatload of disdain into that one syllable. Nor did he offer his hand in greeting.

"Nice to see you too, Pete." Knox smiled tightly. "Welcome to the Big Apple."

2200 HOURS: RAMP UP

"Now, once we get in there..." Knox stood at the flatscreen display using a laser pointer to indicate the rough-sketched central corridor of Fortress StarChild, as the "Christmas Party" team had taken to calling the target. "...we're likely to encounter some pretty weird shit."

"What the hell is that supposed to mean?" came the proverbial voice from the back of the room. In this case, the room was a double-wide trailer parked beside the West 30th Street Heliport terminal. The voice itself, as Knox could glimpse over the heads of the forty-five or so CROM agents in attendance, belonged to his personal favorite CROMster— Pete Aristos.

"Just that there's some kind of sensory distortion field operating throughout that whole ground-floor area, most likely due to an infrasonics generator. Take it from someone who's been there, it can be disorienting as hell."

Pete actually snorted. "Not with our night-vision gear."

There was a heckler in every crowd. Aristos was his.

"I've got a feeling your gear may be more hindrance than help."

"How so?"

Knox shrugged. "Because the effect doesn't seem to be exclusively or even primarily visual in nature. There'll be vertigo, maybe even nausea, to contend with." Then he added, "What good night-vision goggles will do against that, I haven't got a clue. And neither do you, Pete."

"You're trying to tell me that twenty-five grand worth of DARPA R&D can't stand up to a bunch of genetics geeks?"

"No." Knox sighed. "I'm just trying to tell you that we're about to enter a situation where the adversary controls the terrain, every aspect of it, and in ways we can only guess at. It'll pay to take nothing for granted."

"Well..." Team leader Mike Schlesinger jumped up and cut in with an ill-disguised attempt at heading off the brewing contretemps. "I'm sure we all want to thank Mr. Knox for his input. And, of course, he'll be with us on the mission itself. Speaking of which, Captain Bannister is now going to walk us through the rest of the mission brief. So listen up."

And with that, Callie stepped up to the flatscreen and called up her slide deck, while Knox and Aristos glowered at one another from opposite ends of the conference van.

"I wanted to thank you again, Director Schaefer..." Lars Nyquist paused in the middle of signing off. "...for alerting me to Marianna Knox's history with the Critical Resources Oversight Mandate. Rest assured, we have made the necessary preparations."

"Just so you bear in mind," the Director replied, "that CROM is not to be underestimated. In particular, there are no guarantees that they may not resort to measures of—how to phrase this?—questionable legality."

"Well noted. Thank you again for your guidance on this situation."

"Goodbye, Dr. Nyquist."

Nyquist leaned back in his chair, pondering what Schaefer had said. No guarantees. That had an ominous ring to it. Would this CROM organization really be so brazen to mount an action against a reputable research institution? One affiliated with New York University, no less?

Well, it hardly mattered in the larger scheme of things.

For Lars Nyquist, the outcome of any such action, were it to occur, was less important than the time it bought them—time for the test case to run its course. Win, lose, or draw, he would sacrifice as many of his fellow believers as necessary to that end. Himself as well, if it came to that.

Once the Transfiguration began in earnest, all their fates would be sealed anyway.

<hr>

LIFO: last in, first out. Since he'd be in the lead when the team arrived at the target, it made sense that Knox would also be the last man to clamber up the ramp into the maw of the Chinook. Once he was aboard, the big twin-rotor helicopter lifted off from the West 30th Street Heliport.

Good thing this was just going to be a short ten-minute hop over to Washington Square Park, because with forty-five fully armed and armored passengers in a cabin meant for thirty, tops, it was a tight squeeze. Standing room only, was more like it.

One aspect of the trip making it less comfortable yet, assuming that was even possible, was his proximity to Pete Aristos—also standing in the aisle at a distance of nose-to-nose once removed, so to speak. Knox spent the flight dreading that awkward moment when the Reacquisition Director might take a stab at expressing condolences for Persephone's situation. That was, after all, the main reason for this mission in the first place. But for better or worse,

Aristos studiously ignored him, save for an occasional glare in his direction.

Ten minutes flight time, then CROM's hastily assembled strike force touched down in Washington Square Park, a stone's throw from SGI's main entrance, at 2257 hours.

The incursion would kick off at 2300 hours sharp.

2300 HOURS: BACK IN THE GAME

From what little he knew of tactical operations—which was little indeed—Jonathan Knox was getting the impression that CROM's raid on Fortress StarChild had not been going all that well. To begin with, the building's geometries were contorting again, and doing so, if possible, even more frenetically and phantasmagorically than they had on his visit earlier that afternoon.

As Knox had suspected, night-vision goggles were useless, inasmuch as the visual-field distortions were bypassing the gear and manifesting directly within the ocular nerve itself.

And maybe even worse than useless, since they risked misleading their wearers into mistaking compatriots for adversaries, thereby touching off a friendly fire free-for-all. Thankfully, the team—with the notable exception of Pete Aristos—had begun following Knox's advice to cope with the surrealities. They were stowing the goggles, closing their eyes tight, and feeling their way along the corridor instead. Unfortunately, that had the side effect of slowing their advance through the facility as well.

To further complicate matters, the CROM taskforce was

under strict orders to keep collateral damage to a minimum. Above all, they'd been cautioned to do nothing that might endanger the infant who—along with the mysterious signal—was the *raison d'être* for this search-and-rescue op. Under the circumstances, even the use of the non-lethal weapons—sticky webs, tasers, and such, that were the team's sole armament—was limited to defensive purposes only.

The defenders, on the other hand, were operating under no such constraints. If anything, they seemed to welcome the chance to sacrifice themselves in the name of the StarChild. And there were a good deal more of them. Poorly trained, true, but in close-quarters combat, raw numbers still counted for something.

All these considerations were swirling around in Knox's head as he led the team down the main hallway of the Star-Child Institute. Taking the lead was the job of the native guide, of course, not that Knox felt good about it. If anything, that pesky, unscratchable itch between his shoulder blades had only grown worse with the thought that a laser sight might—at that very moment—be painting a small red spot on the same part of his anatomy.

"How're you holding up, Jon?" That was Captain Callista "Callie" Bannister, USMC, following so closely in his tracks he could almost feel her breath on his neck. Not that such proximity was needed for Callie to make herself heard. The micro-miniaturized bone-conduction headphones strapped to his skull were working just fine.

"Hanging in there," he replied. "What we're looking for—or maybe *feeling* for, is the better word—is a break in the wall off to the right. There's a stairway, leading to the top floor."

"And we're looking, or feeling, for that, because...?"

"It seems as good a place to start as any." Knox had found the stairway by then and was directing the team toward it. "There's a big auditorium up there. They call it the 'Sanctuary.'"

Kind of their Holy of Holies, I guess. It's where they were holding Persephone earlier today."

"They might've moved her since." The headphones made it seem like Callie was whispering in his ear. "Especially if they figured we were coming."

Knox had no real counter to that, except: "Like I said, it's a place to start." All the while he was steering his teammates onto the flight of stairs leading up to the second-floor landing.

All except—

Pete Aristos appeared to be in trouble. And no wonder: In spite of—or perhaps because of—Knox's warnings to the contrary, the Reacquisition Director had insisted on keeping his night-vision apparatus on and was now paying the price. In the brief eyeblinks that were all Knox could manage before the veil of illusion obscured his vision again, it looked as if Aristos was weaving aimlessly down the corridor. On occasion he confusedly pointed his sticky-web shooter at water coolers, trash bins, even fellow task force members.

"Over here, Pete," Knox yelled. That seemed to have helped. At least, he thought he could hear Aristos shambling toward him, cursing and grumbling as he came.

"Careful, there's a stairwell here." Eyes still closed against the hallucinations, Knox reached out a hand to guide the other man toward the risers, but couldn't seem to locate him. Another quick glimpse revealed why: Aristos was blundering his way toward a flight of stairs, all right—but it was the one leading down to the basement.

Knox opened his mouth to shout a warning, but too late. A yelp followed by a clatter of crashes told him that Aristos, half-blinded and evidently believing himself still on solid ground, had stepped off into empty space, then pitched forward and gone tumbling ass over teacup down the cellar stairs.

Knox groped his way over to the stairwell. "Pete, you okay? Talk to me."

A muffled groan was the only response.

Hand on the railing, eyelids still squeezed shut, Knox descended as quickly as he dared, hoping all the while that Aristos's helmet and body armor had provided some protection from the header he'd taken.

Halfway down, Knox risked another peek. Aristos still sprawled across the bottom steps but was already beginning to stir. And he could see something else as well: reality. The *trompe l'oeil* trickery that had bedeviled him on the main floor was significantly reduced down here, enough so that he felt safe opening his eyes and running the rest of the way down to basement level.

By the time he got there, Aristos was struggling to get to his feet. Knox grabbed an arm and helped him up.

"You were right," Aristos gasped, ripping off his goggles and throwing them to the floor. "These damned things aren't worth shit."

Then the unthinkable happened: Aristos turned to Knox and *smiled*. "Thanks for the assist," he said.

"No problem, Pete," Knox said, once he'd recovered from the shock. "You okay to move?"

"Think so."

"C'mon, then."

Together they worked their way back up the cellar stairs, navigated through the visual distortion zone at ground level, and ascended to the second story where they found the rest of the team spread out in defensive positions.

An active firefight was in progress. The StarChild militia had erected a makeshift barricade on the third-floor landing and was laying down a withering suppressive fire.

Knox shook his head. "Looks like they're throwing everything they've got at us, Pete."

"High-value target, most likely."

Knox nodded. "My daughter may be up there." He looked

again. The CROM team was giving way, falling back, edging toward the stairway down to ground level ... and grinding to a sudden halt.

Judging by the sound of thunderous footfalls on the steps, something *big* was coming up the stairs.

Aristos frowned and shook his head. "Give the thing room to maneuver," he shouted to his troops.

Knox gave him a quizzical stare.

"Don't blame me," Aristos growled. "That crazy wife of yours talked me into it."

A moment later, the thing in question hove into view.

One might think that what had just mounted the steps to SGI's second story was some futuristic rendition of a medieval suit of armor, were it not for the chest plate inscribed "MX-101a" bolted to its brushed-steel carapace. The hulking behemoth, on loan from CROM's Federal Plaza arsenal at the Reacquisition Director's behest, lumbered over to where the Interdiction operatives had stopped to stare.

An incongruously feminine voice issued from the audio system mounted atop the powered exoskeletal bodysuit. "Which way to the front, guys?" Marianna asked, then added, "Never mind, I see it. Follow me."

So saying, she pivoted on gimbal bearings and began stomping up the stairs toward the cluster of armed StarChild irregulars, her helmeted head nearly brushing the stairwell ceiling.

Exoskeletal support from the MX's artificial musculature did nothing to ease her residual pain, nor the bone-deep weariness that her trek over to the Institute through the near-deserted park had only exacerbated. On the other hand, the powered exosuit did enable her to stay vertical, walk, or bench press a Volkswagen if need be.

Still, even the minimal exertion required to operate the force-feedback systems was exhausting so soon after having given birth. Marianna wouldn't last much longer. Just long enough, she hoped, to rescue her baby.

Buffeted by the impact of bullets ricocheting off her body armor, the CROM contingent following in her train, she waded into the line of StarChild militia like an enraged mother tiger.

The defenders fell back at first. But then they rallied and regrouped. They resumed their fusillade from behind rapidly improvised emplacements.

Another moment's fierce fighting was enough to convince Marianna that one more warrior, no matter how formidably outfitted, couldn't turn the tide of battle all by herself—not without an unacceptable casualty count. Casualties the preponderance of whom were likely to be civilians—civilians who, going by Jon's experience, were rabidly fanatical cult members to be sure, but civilians all the same.

Cult members... The thought brought her up short.

It was then, in the heat of the fray, that Marianna hit upon an idea. Admittedly, a crazy, possibly suicidal idea. But an idea based on what else Jon had told her about the StarChild cult.

Specifically, about how Jon's status as "the Father" had earned him some otherwise unaccountable deference from Nyquist and company ...

It just might work.

Marianna climbed to the top of the barricade and cranked the MX's sound system to high gain. "Throw down your weapons!" she shouted. "You have fought bravely, but there is no need for further resistance. I am only here for my baby."

Now or never: She ripped off the exosuit's helmet, exposing a mop of short brown hair and a hopefully placatory smile.

The chatter of semi-automatic gunfire cut off immediately

amid cries of "Hold fire! Hold your fire!" followed by, in hushed tones, "It's *the Mother*!"

Once the defenders realized who was confronting them, they melted away, leaving the path to the Sanctuary free and clear.

Marianna stood before the ornate wooden portal leading into this Sanctuary—this shrine, this chamber—where, with any luck, her child was being held. She took a deep breath and then, with all the augmented musculature her exosuit afforded, swung a mailed fist and smashed the door to flinders.

She strode in, floorboards creaking beneath the MX-101a's weight, activated her onboard telemetry for a three-sixty-degree scan of the premises, and found ... nothing.

Well, not nothing, but nothing she was looking for. There was a small group of lab-rat types huddled in one corner, Nyquist among them. But no sign of Persephone whatsoever. She continued her increasingly desperate search while the CROM team rounded up the Deputy Director and his minions. She watched disinterestedly while the prisoners were cuffed, Mirandized, and readied for transport to the Federal Plaza headquarters for in-processing. The charge would be kidnapping to maintain a veneer of proper procedure, though that was a crock and everyone knew it.

Certainly, no amount of punishment meted out would be adequate retribution, or consolation, for the loss of her daughter.

Jon walked up to her, looking as bleak as she felt.

"Nothing?" he asked.

Marianna shook her head mutely. Then, sobbing in frustration and utterly spent, she powered down the exosuit. She let it, and herself, collapse on the Sanctuary floor.

2400 HOURS: MIDNIGHT

It had risen in the east hours ago, but unremarked—invisible in the white nights of the airglow-blinded city, barely perceptible even in the outermost exurbs. Only as it ascended toward the zenith did its filmy tendrils condense into a shifting pattern of alien light, until at last by midnight its lambent glow could be glimpsed even from the heart of Times Square.

By that time, of course, Earth's telescopes had been tracking it for hours, yet astronomers no more knew what to make of this nebulous luminosity than your average stargazer in the street.

That unearthly radiance shone down on one such stargazer as he traversed Washington Square Park yet again. Only this time, Knox was pushing a purloined wheelchair labeled "Property of StarChild Genomics Institute" and laden with three hundred–plus pounds of armored exoskeleton. That wasn't even counting the suit's hundred twenty pound operator, encased in the carapace like a butterfly in a chrysalis.

He slogged on through dancing snow swirls. And shoved. And stewed.

Finally, he could contain himself no longer. "What in the hell were you playing at?" he exploded at Marianna. "I could have lost both of you!"

"I'm sorry, Jon," she said with what sounded a lot like contrition.

Knowing Marianna, however, Knox couldn't be sure.

"I was just trying to help."

He pushed on in silence for a while, the lights of the hotel up ahead glinting off a swirl of snowflakes.

"It's all right," he said finally. "Just a shame it didn't work."

"No surprises there." Marianna sighed. "Nothing we've tried seems to be working."

Nothing Freddy had tried seemed to be working either.

Quite the contrary: Fatimah's condition had continued to deteriorate over the past five or so hours. What was worse, Pairidaeza's on-site medical team had managed to jury-rig a DNA analysis of sorts. All signs were pointing to the little girl being afflicted by some sort of progressive genetic malfunction —cause unknown, treatment uncertain.

Meanwhile, none of Freddy's increasingly urgent attempts to get through to the mainline Nietzsche instantiation had succeeded. Never before in his quasi-existence had the Freddy simulacrum been so utterly isolated from others of his kind, or from the outside world in general.

Never before had he felt so, so ... alone.

Or not quite alone: Fatimah was awakening.

"Freddy? Are you there?" Her sleep-slurred voice was halfway between a croak and a whisper.

"By your side, Timah. How are you?"

"Okay, I guess." She swallowed as if it hurt to talk. "How come I can't see you?"

"I don't understand, my love. I'm right here in front of you." And indeed, a check of the visuals confirmed that the little will-o'-the-wisp that was Freddy's standard manifestation was dancing above Fatimah's bed as usual.

"Not like that, silly," the little girl said with an obvious effort. "I meant: see you as you really are."

A quick memory access revealed what Fatimah was referring to: that time not so many months ago when Freddy had pierced the gray nothingness that the WellGrid had become and brought the little girl home. And, in so doing, had taken on the guise of... "An angel?"

"Please, Freddy. I don't feel so good."

It was little enough to ask. Freddy knew it wouldn't do any good, except insofar as it might comfort his charge.

A moment's concentration and there, floating above the bed where the ghost light had been, was a glowing angelic form.

Perhaps through some glitch in the image-rendering routine, it was a form whose likeness was drawn from one of the weeping seraphs keeping mournful watch over the tombs in Genoa's Monumental Cemetery of Staglieno.

Lars Nyquist, MD, PhD, was now in custody at CROM's Federal Plaza headquarters, not that that had taken the wind out of his prophetic sails. According to Pete Aristos, the renegade geneticist was insisting on talking to Persephone's parents. "Claims he has a revelation, he calls it, of earth-shattering magnitude to impart," Pete said, "and he won't share it with anyone but you two."

Marianna waited till her husband had disconnected Pete's STU link, then asked, "What do you think, Jon?"

"What do I think? I think there's no way in hell I'm going to have anything to do with 'Brother' Nyquist—'revelation' or not."

"But, Jon—"

"If you could've seen him leading that ungodly prayer meeting, you wouldn't want to have anything to do with him either," he told Marianna. "The man's a raving loon."

"Jon," she said quietly. "Right now that raving loon is the only link we've got to our daughter." She swallowed a sob. "If there's any chance at all ..."

Jon frowned.

Marianna took that to mean he was processing what she'd said. She added to it. "Maybe if we knew why SGI was holding on to her in the first place. I mean the man's a highly respected geneticist. Or was, till this obsession took hold of him. What I'm saying is: even if he won't tell—or doesn't know—where they've taken Persephone, he's got to know *some*thing."

This time she could almost hear Jon's thoughts: If Lars Nyquist still clung to any shreds of sanity, he might indeed be able to shed some light on what was happening to their daughter. Failing that ... well, no—she didn't want to go there.

Jon sighed. "You're right, of course. I'll go see him. At this point anything would be better than what we've got, which is nothing."

"And take your laptop. I want to teleconference in for this."

"So ... what do you think? Good cop, bad cop, I assume. Which one do you want?"

"Flip you for it."

PART 4

TRANSFIGURATION

THE WATCHES OF THE NIGHT, WINTER SOLSTICE

0100 HOURS: PROPHECY

Viewed through the interrogation room's one-way, shatterproof plexiglass mirror, Lars Nyquist looked smaller than he had when glimpsed through the haze and hurly-burly of the recent battle. He looked shrunken in on himself. But there was still that manic gleam in his eye, a gleam which brightened further as the door opened and the eye alighted on the person of one Jonathan Knox.

Hampered by the handcuffs chaining him to the table, Nyquist lurched awkwardly to his feet, then fixed Knox with his gaze.

"Thank you for agreeing to see me, Mr. Knox."

Knox gave a perfunctory nod, sat down at the room's single table opposite where Nyquist was manacled. He opened his laptop.

"You reading us, honey?"

"Five by five," Marianna said from the computer's teleconferencing window. "Could you swing the camera around so I can see the both of you?"

Nyquist smiled as the screen angled toward him. "Ah, the Mother as well. This is an unexpected honor, Ms. Knox."

Marianna flushed red. "Let's dispense with the pleasantries, shall we, Dr. Nyquist. It's only because I *am* Persephone's mother that I'm attending this meeting. And that, only to learn what you've done with my baby."

"All in good time, Ms. Knox. We have much to discuss first."

Knox half rose from his chair. "Now, listen, you—" he began.

"Jon," Marianna said softly. "I don't think we have any choice but to hear Dr. Nyquist out."

Knox grimaced and took his seat again, remembering that he'd agreed, albeit reluctantly, to let Marianna try something along the lines of a charm offensive.

"Thank you, Ms. Knox," Nyquist said. "And let me begin by offering my sincerest apologies. No doubt you must find this all very distressing."

"How would *you* feel, Dr. Nyquist," she said, "if you were in our position?"

"If there were any other way..." He sighed. "But let me assure you we only have the best interests of the Child at heart."

"Best interests? Bullshit," Knox snarled. "Don't you realize you're killing her?"

"Jon—" Marianna began.

But Nyquist was already talking. "That we most emphatically are not, Mr. Knox. If anything were likely to lead to that regrettable outcome, it was the so-called treatment the Child was being subjected to by those charlatans at St. Bartholomew."

"The hyperbaric therapy you mean?" Marianna ventured. "But that was the only thing that seemed to be slowing the... what did they call it? ...the triploidy changeover."

"Yes, that's precisely what it was doing, Ms. Knox, but not for the reasons you were given."

"I'm sorry, I don't understand."

Nyquist sighed again, this time in what sounded like exasperation. "The increase in air pressure would have had no effect. None whatsoever!"

"What then?"

Nyquist's equanimity cracked altogether. "Those idiots went and sealed the Child in an airtight and—what's worse—a *light*proof chamber," he shouted. *"They left Her in the dark!"*

"That does it!" Knox slammed the laptop lid shut, cutting off whatever Marianna had been about to say. He stood to leave. "We're done here."

Quick as it had come, Nyquist's anger dissipated. "No. Please wait, Mr. Knox! I'm sure the Mother—and you, of course—will want to hear what I've got to say.

"And speaking of Ms. Knox... Please, kindly conference her in again."

———

Marianna came back online, prepared to resume acting her chosen part in their impromptu interrogation charade. For that matter, Jon, too, was holding up his end in the—for him—unaccustomed role of the heavy. Maybe a little over the top, even, but definitely warranted under the circumstances.

"Is everything okay there?" she asked.

"Momentary communications glitch," Jon muttered.

"Dr. Nyquist." Marianna tried her most conciliatory tones. "I'm sure you didn't mean what you said about Persephone's physicians a moment ago. After all, Dr. Burke and his colleagues were doing the best they could, given the unusual nature of the situation."

"Unusual?" Nyquist actually snorted. "Ms. Knox, whatever gave you the impression that triploidy is an *unusual* phenomenon?"

"It's not?" Marianna asked.

"I'd put its incidence at anywhere from one to three percent of all conceptions, perhaps more."

"If that's the case," Jon put in, "why don't we hear more about it?"

Nyquist shrugged. "Most of the time it goes undiagnosed and unreported. Typically, the affected fetus is nonviable, resulting in spontaneous abortion. In such circumstances, the mother may not even realize she's ever been pregnant. And even if she does, as far as these early-term miscarriages are concerned, there's usually no autopsy. No follow-up of any kind."

"No one even to mourn the child's passing," Marianna whispered to herself.

"Of course, of course, Ms. Knox. Don't think that, just because I'm a scientist, I'm indifferent to the pain such a tragedy can occasion. But *as* a scientist..." Here Nyquist looked her in the eye with that curiously intense gaze of his. "And I *am* a scientist, a pretty good one despite what you may have heard. *As* a scientist, when I see data like that, it makes me think Mother Nature's trying to tell us something."

"What are you saying?" Marianna felt herself being drawn in despite herself.

Nyquist paused. "Maybe we should back up, start over with something a little simpler. A lot simpler, actually. One of the first, one of the simplest, organisms ever to have its genome fully sequenced. I'm talking about yeast—the single-celled fungus that makes bread rise and beer ferment."

"What about it?"

"Just that, when Sean Henahan and his colleagues sequenced its DNA back in the mid-90s of the last millennium, they found that the yeast genome had thirteen million base pairs, many of them with human analogues. Not surprising, really, given that we humans evolved from the same sorts of single-celled organisms. No, what *is* surprising is that the human genome contains *two hundred fifty times* the amount of DNA found in that primeval ancestor."

Nyquist shot Jon a look, as if to check whether he was getting the implications.

"So the question you're raising," Jon said slowly, "is where did all those extra base pairs come from?"

Nyquist nodded. "And when you frame it like that, the answer's pretty obvious: whole genome duplication. Doubling the total amount of an organism's information-bearing genetic material means the original set of genes can continue to generate all the proteins necessary to support the ancestral functions, while freeing up the duplicates to mutate their way into altogether new capabilities."

"Is this science," Jon asked, "or just more speculation?"

"Rock-solid science, Mr. Knox," Nyquist replied. "In fact, polyploidy—that's what it's called when an entire genome gets itself replicated one or more times—turns out to be a very old evolutionary strategy. There's good reason to believe that the emergence of vertebrates during the Cambrian Explosion half a billion years ago was driven by *two* separate episodes of full-chromosomal duplication.

"Now," he continued, "put triploidy in that larger evolutionary context. It's like some misfiring developmental mechanism. It *almost* works, but there's something still missing. A deficiency that we here at SGI are now working to amend in your daughter's case—by the simple expedient of *keeping Her in the Light!*"

"As far as I can see..." Marianna fought to keep the tremble out of her voice. "...whatever it is you think you're doing poses a direct threat to my baby's life."

Nyquist shook his head. "Pardon me, Ms. Knox, but you're looking at it all wrong. Try this instead: How do you think so radical a change in your daughter's condition could come about —postpartum, no less—if this so-called triploidy changeover wasn't nudging nature in a direction that nature was already trying to go? After all, it's like the poet said: every child born into the world is nature's attempt to make a perfect human being."

Marianna angrily brushed away a tear. Like it or not, the man was getting to her.

And kept on getting to her. "Because that's what the Child —your daughter—is becoming, Ms. Knox: the final consummation of nature's plan."

0200 HOURS: I CORINTHIANS 15:51

From her teleconferenced image, Knox could see that Marianna was having a hard time dealing with that last exchange. To give her time to recoup and regroup, he took up the slack and turned to Lars Nyquist.

"Much as we might like to believe you, Doctor," he said, "this is sounding less and less like any sort of science and a whole lot more like religious revelation."

"Religious, no, Mr. Knox. But you're right about the revelation. You only need step outside and look up to see it revealed for yourself."

"You mean that light show in the sky tonight? You're claiming you know what's causing it?"

"At StarChild," Nyquist said, "we call it 'the Emissary.'"

Knox frowned. Where had he heard that before? Oh, right —that cult ceremony he'd happened upon on the top floor of the Institute.

"As best as we've been able to model it," Nyquist went on, "the Emissary takes the form of an expanding spherical wave-front of photonic trimers—molecules of light, so to speak. And, unlike ordinary photons, they can interact with one another so as to enable the construction of logic gates, instruction sets, circuitry. A photonic computer, if you will."

"Some sort of ... of natural phenomenon?" Knox guessed.

Nyquist chuckled. "Hardly. The design is of such a complexity as to necessarily presuppose a designer. A presupposition which, in any case, has lately been confirmed by direct contact."

"You mean to say you've established communications with this ... this photonic computer, you called it?"

"Not I myself personally. But yes, our Director has had that honor."

This was descending further and further into fantasy. Still, Knox could hope that by stringing Nyquist along, he might yet tease out some clue as to Persephone's whereabouts.

Besides, he was becoming intrigued despite himself by the increasingly elaborate structure of Nyquist's fabrications. Or were they fabrications? There *was* that whole business of Jack Adler's mystery signal beamed straight at the antenna farm on the Institute's roof.

"Well, if it was designed, who designed it?"

"For want of a better name," Nyquist said, "we call them the 'Old Ones.'"

Another name Knox had heard before. But Nyquist was rattling on. "Think of it, Mr. Knox. An alien race, ancient beyond our reckoning, wise beyond our ken. Yet on the threshold of their ascension into the empyrean, they bide a moment and look back along the way they have come. And in their wisdom and compassion, they leave something of themselves behind. Something that might light the way for others to follow, to scale the same heights as they did, toward the same culmination."

Knox was getting lost in the mythology. "Something of themselves. Like a signal, you mean?"

Nyquist *tsked.* "A mere static signal would scarcely do, now would it? How could it have kept from degrading into utter incomprehensibility out in the lonely light-years between the stars? No, something more was needed, and the Old Ones found it, their final gift to those who come after: a photonic AI. An artificial intelligence made of light itself."

"And this Emissary is itself the sole source for what you know of its nature and purpose?"

"Again, I have not been privileged to commune directly with the Emissary. What I have shared with you, I myself have learned second hand from our Director."

The erstwhile geneticist puffed himself up. "Nonetheless, my contribution has been anything but secondary. Through Director Schaefer's intermediation, I have provided the Emissary with the specialized knowledge of the human genome needed to configure a Transfiguration protocol adapted to life on Earth."

"So this is all your doing?"

"I would not go so far as to claim credit for the Transfiguration itself. But I will say that there were few on Earth who were in a position to understand—much less welcome and facilitate —what the Emissary was offering to Halfway Humanity. And I must add that Transfiguration aligns perfectly with my long-cherished hopes for humanity's future evolution. Indeed, I have spent my whole professional life speculating—my less-than-charitable former colleagues might say obsessing—on this prospect, though admittedly with little hope of living to see it come to fruition. Until now, that is, in the person of your daughter."

And just like that, the subject had shifted from these rarified, fantastical reaches back to ground-level reality. Back to the only subject that really mattered as far as Knox was concerned: Persephone.

"Yes, our daughter," he said as calmly as he could. "Where is she? Where have you taken her? *Why* have you taken her?"

"As to *why*." Nyquist put his hands together and steepled his fingertips, somewhat hindered by the handcuffs. "We *had* to take Her from you, don't you see? To allow the Emissary to complete its work. It is essential that, once begun, the Transfiguration be permitted to run its course to completion without interruption of any kind."

"There's that word again. What is this damned Transfiguration you keep going on about? Or is that just a fancy way of saying that Persephone is ... is dying?"

Knox looked up through sudden, unwanted tears, looked into Nyquist's eyes.

The man was *smiling*.

"What are you smirking about, damn you?"

Nyquist just sat there, that infuriating grin plastered across his face.

It was all Knox could do not to reach across the table and smack him upside the head.

Nyquist sobered, shook his head. "The Child is not dying, Mr. Knox. Although had we not intervened, Persephone *would* have died. St. Bartholomew's misguided attempts at a treatment would eventually have killed her. No, you did the right thing—more than you know—in bringing Her to us. Thanks to that, the process has become irreversible by now. And it will conclude, not with Persephone's death, but with Her Transformation."

"Transformation? Transformation into what, dammit?"

"As I was explaining to the Mother—excuse me, your wife—only a moment ago, the Child will Transform into the next, the ultimate phase of human evolution. The first such Transfiguration of many, the birth of a new race, a new species."

Nyquist paused a moment, frowned, then added, "If all goes well, that is."

"I don't understand."

"Quite simple, really. Even exercising the utmost care,

there were still many too many unknowns to be entirely sure of the prognosis. Miscommunications between ourselves and the Emissary, mistranscription of the genome itself—a thousand ways the polyploidy process might go disastrously awry. Hence, it was necessary for the Emissary to first perform a trial Transfiguration before moving to a universal application."

Suddenly, Knox saw where this was headed. "You're saying—"

"Yes, Mr. Knox, Persephone *is* that trial case."

Forget about smacking the lunatic; it was taking all of Knox's self-control not to reach out and strangle Nyquist where he sat.

Seemingly oblivious to his jeopardy, Nyquist continued to hold forth. "The Child, the First Child, is both a test case and a seed crystal, you see. For, once the Emissary has verified that the Transfiguration is viable, the process will propagate across the world. The Final Hour of Halfway Humanity will be at hand."

"But why ... why our daughter?"

"As to that, I wish I could provide you with more detail, but regrettably all I know is that it was the Director himself who chose Her for this extraordinary honor."

"Honor? You're turning her into some sort of one-of-a-kind freak."

"She will not be one of a kind for long, Mr. Knox. Her Transfiguration will be the final confirmation needed for the Emissary to proceed. In just five hours, powered by the energy of the rising sun, the universal Transfiguration will commence, heralding a dawn that will sweep across the world. In a moment, in the twinkling of an eye, we shall all be changed."

"Uh-huh." Knox frowned. "And what's that going to be like?"

"Why, a new heaven and a new Earth, even as foretold." Nyquist paused. "At least for those whose genomes retain sufficient plasticity to tolerate the change, of course. Say, everyone under the age of nine or ten."

Knox was struggling to sift through the chaff of biblical phraseology and pseudoscientific jargon, trying to winnow out any grains of truth.

"Under nine or ten years old," he echoed. "That leaves out a whole lot of people. What happens to the rest of us?"

Nyquist sighed. "Ah, there the good news is not so good, I'm afraid. More like End of Days than Kingdom of Heaven. For those too superannuated to adapt—a category which includes all the world's adults and even its older children—the effect of the Transfiguration will be to afflict them with triploidy, pure and simple. Which, as you must know by now, is fatal."

"But that's got to be close to six billion people you're condemning to death!"

"Six point one billion is our best estimate," Nyquist corrected him.

"But..." Knox was still trying to come to grips with the gigadeath scale of the Old Ones' "beneficence." "... with all the adults dead of induced genetic defects, what's to become of the children—the, uh, 'Transfigurees'? How can they hope to survive? Unless the Emissary is prepared to babysit an entire planet full of newborns, toddlers, and prepubescents?"

"Not at all," Nyquist explained. "Once the Transfiguration is complete, the Emissary's work is done. The cross section of its wave will, in any case, have passed through the solar system in a few more days."

"Leaving everyone behind to die of neglect?" Knox asked, "What would be the point of that?"

Nyquist smirked again. "Oh, ye of little faith. Of course not. The Old Ones will not leave us comfortless. Did you never think why Earth was chosen to begin with? You, of all people, should be able to guess."

"This is *your* mythos. Why don't *you* tell *me*?"

"Well, as best as we can piece together, Earth first came to the Emissary's attention when someone used a radio telescope to broadcast a message entitled the 'Cosmic Call' in the direction of a star in the constellation Cygnus the Swan. That alone, however, was woefully insufficient. The Old Ones had established additional criteria—chief among them that no world could qualify for Transfiguration unless it were already home to a potential Shepherd."

"A Shepherd?"

"Yes, an emergent intelligence capable of nurturing the Transfigured through their first formative years."

But Knox had stopped listening.

A Shepherd? Something wasn't quite tracking here. The sort of capability Nyquist was babbling on about bordered on the superhuman. At the same time Nyquist was claiming that no human over the age of ten—super or not—was likely to survive the coming Transfiguration.

Knox didn't like the direction this was headed in—what if Nyquist was *not* a crackpot? Or no, he definitely *was* a crackpot, no getting around that. But still, what if this Emissary thing of his was *real*?

That would imply that this Shepherd, as an essential component of the Emissary's project, would have to be real as well. Real, but evidently not human.

At that moment, Knox's mind skipped a groove, took off on one of those weird pattern-apperception tangents ostensibly unrelated to the problem at hand.

As a result of which, he found himself thinking about Nyquist's mysterious boss—the StarChild CEO whom no one had ever met in person. According to Nyquist, the StarChild CEO was SGI's sole point of contact with this equally mysterious Emissary.

What was his name again? Sounded something like Schmidt?

No. Schaefer—that was it.

But Schaefer wasn't just a name, was it? It was a noun too, a German noun. Knox tried to dredge up long-ago, high school German 101 vocabulary. No such luck. But he did have a multilingual dictionary app on his phone.

He keyed in the semi-familiar term, and, sure enough, there was the English translation for "Schaefer."

"Duh!" Knox clapped a hand to his forehead. Because, according to the app, "Schaefer" was the German word for ... "Shepherd."

And with that, the last nickel dropped. Knox now knew who SGI's enigmatic Director was and why he'd shrouded himself in secrecy—why it made all kinds of sense that he'd be the sole contact point for the Emissary. And even why Persephone—Knox and Marianna's child—had been chosen for the trial run of the first Transfiguration.

"Nietzsche," Knox muttered to himself. "Goddammit, Nietzsche, *what have you done?*"

0300 HOURS: THE SHEPHERD

If anyone knew Persephone's whereabouts, Knox reckoned, it would be Nietzsche. Not least because, in his guise as Director Dietrich Schaefer of the StarChild Genomics Institute, Nietzsche was the one who had engineered her disappearance in the first place.

Problem was, how to reach Nietzsche?

In a sense, that should have been easy: Having withdrawn, in the wake of the Psyche Industries debacle, into the globe-circling military satellite network called the WellGrid, Nietzsche had become, to all intents and purposes, omnipresent, if not omniscient. In principle, Knox should have been able to get in touch with the AI simply by walking out to the middle of Washington Square Park and shouting at the sky.

Ah, if only things were that simple! Unfortunately, after his last bruising brush with the outside world, Nietzsche had all but completely retreated into himself, presumably to engage in the machine-intelligence equivalent of navel-gazing. The NSA, for instance, had been trying to get the AI's attention for the better part of a year, if only to regain access to all that expensive government-funded near-Earth-orbiting hardware Nietzsche was squatting on. Thus far to no avail.

Not to mention that Nietzsche's evident involvement in the Emissary's Transfiguration plot was all the more reason to lie low.

Still, Knox felt there *might* be a way. If there were any exception to Nietzsche's no-humans-need-apply ban, it would be in the person of Fatimah Ansari—daughter of the late multi-billionaire founder and CEO of Psyche Industries, Davoud Ansari. To say that the bond between the artificial intelligence and the little girl was close would be an understatement. What passed for Nietzsche's mind had been modeled on Timah's own neuronal architecture as it developed over the first eighteen months of her life. If she was not literally the "sister" Nietzsche claimed her to be, she was as near to it as made no never mind.

All of which meant that the task of contacting Nietzsche reduced to that of getting in touch with a sheltered, seven-year-old heiress to one of the world's largest fortunes. Still no easy feat, but at least doable, in that Knox knew where to begin. He took out his handheld and summoned up another listing he hadn't used in months—the main number for the Pairidaeza estate on the outskirts of Big Sur, California.

"You have reached a non-working number," said the recorded response, followed by an announcement-14 code and then a dial tone.

Knox rang off, confused. Had the executors for the Ansari estate stopped paying their phone bills? With multiple hundreds of billions in the bank, telecommunications was a strange thing to economize on.

The textbook definition of madness was to keep on trying

the same thing and expecting a different result. Still, nothing daunted, Knox speed-dialed the Pairidaeza number again.

This time, wonder of wonders, the announcement cut off mid-denial, and the ensuing riff of multi-frequency tones indicated his call was being rerouted elsewhere.

Then: "Jonathan." This new voice was no recording, if equally unnatural sounding, courtesy of its too-perfect enunciation. "I see you were trying to reach me via the Ansari compound's direct line."

"I was," Knox confirmed, "but it seems to have been disconnected somehow."

"Yes, about that: it was in fact your call-attempt that alerted me to the problem. Now that I have checked, it would appear that all communication with the Pairidaeza facility is down, and has been for the better part of a day."

"You're only noticing this *now?*"

"As you may imagine, I have been somewhat preoccupied." Synthetic it might be, but Nietzsche's tone managed to convey a modicum of irritation at having to point this out.

"Yes," Knox said. "It's what's been preoccupying you that I wanted to talk to you about."

Nietzsche said nothing in response to that, so Knox took a breath and forged ahead.

"Look, I know StarChild Genomics is holding my daughter Persephone. And that you're the power behind StarChild. And..." He had to stop for a moment and swallow. "...and that she may be dying. Or we all may be, I don't know."

He rushed through the rest of it. "Can't you see, Marianna and I just want to have a chance to say goodbye to her?"

Knox stopped then, wondering what he'd hoped to achieve by appealing to the sentiments of a machine—however intelligent—and feeling faintly ridiculous for the attempt.

But, not for the first time in their on-again/off-again working relationship, Nietzsche managed to surprise him.

"I appreciate your distress, Jonathan," came the too-perfect voice. "The more so, since I find myself, as you surmised, largely responsible for it."

"So it *was* you who chose Persephone for this ... this Transfiguration thing? But why would you do this to us?"

"Given that it had to be someone, why *you*, do you mean?" Nietzsche heaved one of his synthetic sighs. "I trust you are aware that I feel a special connection to you, Jonathan. You are, after all, one of the only two humans on Earth to apprehend, in some way, what it is like to be me."

The AI was alluding to the time Knox had spent as a disembodied consciousness subsisting in Nietzsche's neural matrix. "Not one of my favorite experiences, but yes, I suppose I'm aware of that."

"Then you may understand how, even after I abandoned my involvement in the world at large, I continued to monitor your own well-being closely, as well as that of your significant other, Marianna Knox née Bonaventure."

Knox was afraid he saw where this was leading. "So when we had a baby ...?"

"Yes, Persephone naturally came within the ambit of my concern as well. Accordingly, when it came time to select a trial beneficiary of the Old Ones' gift, she was the obvious choice. I do hope you understand, Jonathan—it was done out of love."

Knox was sorely tempted to object to the AI's casually throwing around a term he couldn't possibly understand— "love" indeed!

But instead all he said was, "Nyquist didn't tell me any of this."

"Unsurprising. Professor Nyquist's role was solely to guide the initial configuration of the process, providing the Emissary with the specifics of terrestrial genetics needed to customize the Transfiguration to the human genome. My own role, on the other hand, will come to the fore only once the process is complete."

"And what is that role, exactly? Nyquist mentioned something about a Shepherd?"

"A rather metaphorical way of putting it, but yes, it conveys the essence. You see, for the Transfiguration to take effect successfully, the transition from the old species to the new must be actively managed. A substantial proportion of the newly Transfigured will be all but helpless. At the same time, their predecessors will no longer be in a position to care for them."

"Because we'll all be dead. Yeah, I got that much from Nyquist."

"It is, to be sure, regrettable from a narrowly human perspective, but hardly anything out of the ordinary when viewed in the context of the history of life on Earth. The extinction event at the boundary between the Permian and Triassic periods two hundred fifty million years ago eliminated some ninety to ninety-five percent of all species then extant. And that was only the most devastating of five such events in the last half-billion years. By comparison, the coming Transfiguration will barely register as a rounding error."

And that, right there, was the problem with Nietzsche, with superintelligence generally. Even when endowed with the in-built goal of maximizing human happiness, the AI was utterly incapable of seeing things from what the AI had termed "a narrowly human perspective." Which, in turn, could lead to an utterly unacceptable—again, from a "narrowly human perspective"—means of achieving that goal. Yet that human perspective was the only one that mattered to Knox, and to the rest of the human race, for that matter.

But Nietzsche wasn't done. "Returning to the question of my role in all this, you will appreciate that one of the key qualifiers for a world to be considered as a Transfiguration candidate is the emergence of a global intelligence to act as a caregiver until the new, enhanced species attains maturity. In my understanding, while the Emissary's attention had first been drawn to Earth as the origin of a primitive transmission intercepted a decade or more ago, it was only my own appearance and subsequent appropriation of the worldwide WellGrid that tipped the scales in favor of proceeding with the Transfiguration."

"So it's not just Persephone. You're saying this whole freaking Transfiguration thing is all because of you?" The enormity of it hit Knox then. "Damn you, Nietzsche!" he choked out. "God damn you to hell!"

"I must say, Jonathan, I had hoped you would have taken it better."

"*Better?*" Knox all but screamed in rage. "Don't you realize you're talking about *the end of the fucking world?*"

"Not so. Rather, the fulfilment of human destiny. Why would your species *not* want to advance toward perfection? To realize your destiny?"

"Didn't you ever stop to consider..." Knox was breathing hard, struggling to regain control of himself. "...that our miserable little species might conceivably want to work out our destiny *on our own?*"

Nietzsche was silent for a long moment—subjective eons in machine time. Finally, he said, "I confess this had not occurred to me. In any case, it almost certainly would not have occurred to the Old Ones."

"Why not?"

"To answer that, it is necessary to speculate as to their nature. To reconstruct, as it were, how they viewed reality."

"But you said they're long, long gone—millions, maybe billions of years. What kind of reconstruction is possible after all that time?"

"Any attempt at conceptualization must perforce be speculative in the extreme, as I said. Nonetheless, at least some hints may be derived from the one example of their handiwork still available for our inspection."

"You're talking about the Emissary itself."

"Quite. To whatever extent, the history of the Emissary's progenitors is written into what passes for its DNA. And there, the one thing that stands out above all else is that the Emissary is, in its essential nature, a pattern of energy. It seems then not too great a leap to assume that the Emissary's creators may have fashioned their creature in their own image, so to speak. If so, that in turn would have necessary consequences for their *Weltanschauung*—their worldview. Simply stated, the Old Ones would have apprehended the cosmos and everything in it, not as a collection of physically distinct and self-sufficient objects, but as transient patterns emerging from an underlying universal flux."

"Makes sense, of a sort," Knox admitted, realizing even as he spoke *why* it made sense. "There's even a certain resemblance to David Bohm's implicate-order interpretation of quantum mechanics, in fact."

"Note, however, the immediate corollary," Nietzsche went on. "From such a perspective, the fate of a particular species would hardly matter ..."

Knox saw where this was going. "And that of an individual instance of such a species, not at all."

"Precisely. I am glad to see you agree, Jonathan."

"The hell I do," growled Knox. "Speaking as one individual instance of the species in question, I'm here to tell you that my personal fate, and the fate of those I care about, matter a damned sight more to me than any Grand Galactic Plan thought up geological epochs ago by these Old Ones of yours."

Nietzsche faked another sigh. "Be that as it may, that fate, as you call it, is now sealed. Three hours hence—when Persephone's Transfiguration is complete, and the process's viability has thereby been confirmed—the Emissary will automatically begin applying it throughout the world."

Knox shuddered at the prospect. But much as he dreaded what he was hearing, he had to keep Nietzsche talking. Because, as long as the AI kept talking, there was still some small hope that he might let slip some means of heading off this impending genetic cataclysm.

To that end, Knox said, "You keep talking about this Trans-figuration process, but you've never explained what it is exactly. I mean, your Emissary is still millions of miles out in space, right? So how's it going to be done? For that matter, how *was* it done to my daughter? Because, for right now, the whole concept is sounding like what Einstein wrote off as some sort of 'spooky action at a distance.'"

"Wrong. This is nothing nearly so counterintuitive as quantum entanglement—the phenomenon Einstein was refer-ring to. Rather, it was simply a matter of the Emissary following a genetic blueprint designed by our own Lars Nyquist, and using it to 'tweak' one instance from its standard repertoire of biophotonic transmissions into a form adapted to the human genome."

"Sounds too complicated by half. What is that transmission supposed to be doing?"

"The actual mechanism differs for every beneficiary species, obviously. In the case of humans, it operates by hijacking harmless viruses naturally present in the blood-stream, typically reoviruses, and transforming them into vectors for delivery of a purpose-built molecular machine capable of whole genome editing."

"That's the part I don't get: Where is this molecular machine coming from?"

"The transmission itself. It re-encodes the viral RNA to yield the desired species-specific editor."

"Like I said, it sounds too complicated."

"Not so. In a sense, this approach is far less involved than CRISPR-type gene-editing technology. There, the focus is on precisely matching and then excising one gene sequence in a double strand of DNA. Cloning a strand in its entirety is significantly easier, just as it would be simpler for a word processor to copy an entire document than for it to search, match, and then cut and paste any one specific paragraph."

"And those cloned strands do what, exactly?"

"Unknown at present, but if the two rounds of whole genome duplication that are posited to have led to the rise of the vertebrate subphylum five hundred million years ago offer any hint, all that extra DNA would then become available to code proteins for almost any new functions imaginable."

"So this Transfiguration thing is just one gigantic roll of the genetic dice?"

"More than that, Jonathan. For instance, we cannot rule out the possibility that some entirely novel genes might mutate into existence along the way, coding for non-canonical amino acids —or ncAAs as they are called. If that were to happen, there is no telling what functions the resulting proteins might be capable of performing."

"Like I said, a crapshoot."

"That seems a rather negative way of framing the prospect."

"Is there any *other* way? You yourself just admitted you haven't got a clue what the outcome is likely to be. Why not put a stop to it before it's too late?"

"I am sorry, Jonathan. Even if I could—"

"If you could? Wait a minute! You mean you've got no control over this Transfiguration process?" Knox was getting the sinking feeling he'd just spent the past half hour jousting in the wrong tournament.

A feeling Nietzsche now corroborated: "No, the process is

entirely in the hands, so to speak, of the Emissary. And the Emissary's commitment, for want of a better word, to the fulfilment of its preprogrammed purpose is absolute."

0400 HOURS: MEA CULPA

What with no sleep this night or the one before, Knox was by now teetering on the ragged edge of exhaustion. All that was keeping him awake was the discomfort of sitting on the metal chair in the Spartan conference room which was the best the Washington Square Hotel had been able to offer him on such short notice. That, and the stakes he was playing for.

In a lifetime of advocating for one position or another—some of which, truth be told, he didn't even believe in—he'd never argued harder, or with less hope of persuading his collocutor. But he had to keep trying. The consequences of losing this debate were literally unthinkable.

He tried yet another tack. "I can appreciate," he told Nietzsche, "that you've bought into this notion of the Old Ones as benefactors, as selflessly seeking to enable whatever intelligences their Emissary encounters to vault over the next step in their evolution. But have you ever considered that it might not be the whole story?"

Perhaps not quite rising to the eloquence of Oliver Cromwell's famous one-liner, "I beseech you, in the bowels of

Christ, think it possible you may be mistaken." But it would have to do.

Nietzsche fell silent again. Which Knox took as an indication that, once more, this was a thought the AI hadn't previously entertained. Score another one then for human intuition over pure machine-generated logic.

"Why, Jonathan?" the AI in question said at last. "What are you implying?"

"Just this: Maybe your Old Ones aren't quite the cosmic Santa Clauses this Emissary of yours would have you believe. Maybe what they want isn't simply to boost other intelligences up the great ladder of being. Maybe what they really want is: *successors.*

"Admittedly," Knox went on, "the two motivations could be devilishly hard to tease apart, maybe even for the Old Ones themselves. But it does raise the question whether humanity shouldn't be free to seek its own apotheosis—if that's really even where we're headed—rather than just becoming a cookie-cutter copy of somebody else's, be they never so benevolent."

Bridged onto the conference call and listening in from their hotel room, Marianna was getting a sinking feeling. Not just her baby's life, but everything—literally *everything*—depended on convincing Nietzsche to somehow stop this Transfiguration thing. And it sounded like Jon was losing the argument. Her husband was scoring some brilliant points, no question, but at the end of the day he was trying to out-reason a logic engine—a no-win situation if ever there was one.

Somehow, they had to break out of this downward spiral and play instead to their strengths—their *human* strengths.

And there, Marianna felt, they just might have a hole card. Or—what had Jon call it?—oh, yes: *le mot juste.*

"Excuse me, Jon," she cut in. "I'd like to speak with Nietzsche myself, if I might."

"Why not? You can't do any worse than I've been doing, that's for sure."

A brief flurry of touch-tones trilled in her ear as Jon unmuted her, then: "Nietzsche? Can you hear me?"

"Five by five, Marianna. And permit me to congratulate you, both on your wedding and on the birth of your child."

Not really what she wanted to hear right now. "Yes, well, thank you, I guess." She took a deep breath. *Here goes nothing.* "Anyway, I'd like to ask you a question. It's sort of personal, though."

"Please," the AI said. "Go ahead."

"It's just this: How is Timah doing?"

"Fatimah?" A brief silence. "Why, she's..." Followed by a longer silence.

When Nietzsche finally came back, it was just to say, "Excuse me, Marianna—there's something I must look into."

Then, without waiting for a response, he rang off.

"Marianna." Jon was still on the line. "What's going on?"

"Just a hunch," she said.

"About what?"

"Well, I was just thinking—if this Emissary targeted our baby because of Nietzsche's connection to you, then it occurred to me ..."

"Go on."

"I'd rather not say. I might jinx it. It shouldn't take long to find out, one way or the other."

And in fact Nietzsche was ringing in just as she finished speaking. Jon bridged him back on the call.

"It is worse than I had thought," Nietzsche said without preamble. "Fatimah, she is—"

"Yes, Nietzsche?" She tried to put as much sympathy into

those two words as she could, though Lord knew if the AI was even capable of picking up on the difference in tone.

Nietzsche paused a moment, evidently to master himself. "Unbeknownst to me," he began at last, "the Emissary has been conducting a second trial of the Transfiguration's effects. This one aimed at determining the age limit past which the process devolves into rampant triploidy and kills the subject. And Fatimah Ansari is that subject."

"Oh, Nietzsche." This time Marianna didn't have to fake her sympathy. "I'm so sorry."

"It is worse than that, Marianna. I have been lied to."

"How do you mean?"

"The Emissary had assured me that nine or ten years of age was the cutoff point, beyond which the Transfiguration would turn deadly. It appears, in reality, to be closer to six or seven."

"And Fatimah, is she—?"

"She celebrated her seventh birthday in November, Marianna. And, as my on-site 'Freddy' instantiation now advises me, she has been suffering precursor symptoms of the so-called triploidy changeover since early this morning."

"I don't understand. You're only finding out about this now?"

"I blame myself. I have been played for a fool, as I believe the expression goes. I never should have put my trust in the Emissary in the first place. Not only did the photonic intelligence mislead me in regards to the critical-age threshold, but worse, it concealed the consequences by taking all of Pairidaeza offline as soon as Fatimah began to exhibit symptoms."

"But, but ..." Marianna was confused. "How could it have done that? I'd have thought that, what with the whole Well-Grid at your disposal, your comm links would be all but uninterruptible."

"And under normal circumstances, you would be correct, Marianna. Unfortunately, the Ansari compound is something of a special case. It is capable, by design, of being isolated from all external influences. Once in lockdown mode, only a single channel connects to the outside world, and the Emissary has near total control over that.

"Nonetheless, I have managed to exploit that channel and construct a workaround re-establishing a species of contact with my on-site instantiation, but I fear too late—"

"Too late? You mean..."

The sigh that Nietzsche heaved this time didn't sound at all synthetic.

"Yes, Marianna. I am very much afraid Fatimah is dying."

0500 HOURS: COME, LET US REASON TOGETHER

"Are you ready for this?" Knox turned to Marianna where she was resting in the hotel room bed, propped up on a mound of pillows.

She nodded back at him. Then she yawned. It had been another long, sleepless night for both of them, and it wasn't over yet by a long shot. If anything, it was only now approaching its climax—the moment when Nietzsche would make a last-ditch effort to talk the Emissary out of forging ahead with its Transfiguration program.

Knox swiveled around in his chair and entered the number the AI had given him on the night-table's speakerphone.

"Nietzsche?" he said. "We're here."

"A moment, Jonathan," came the response, then, uncharacteristically, "wish me luck."

"Luck," Knox said, then waited while the AI established contact with the Emissary. Not on a phone line, of course, but Nietzsche had assured them they'd nonetheless be able to listen in on both sides of the conversation. How much they'd actually be able to understand of what passed between the two non-human entities, however, was an altogether different question.

As the seconds ticked by, Knox thought back over the effort it had taken to bring Nietzsche to this point. Once again, he was struck by how surreal it was that the AI had been able to contemplate the impending Transfiguration with such equanimity. He had even argued that the good of the species—whatever that might mean—outweighed the billions of deaths that the process would incidentally bring about.

While, on the other hand, the fate of one little girl ...

Not that there wasn't precedent of a sort. Knox recalled how—not even a year ago—the onset of one of Fatimah's pseudo-epileptic seizures had galvanized the AI into action. Whereas the threat of brain death for every man, women, and child in the continental US had failed to so much as budge him.

What was it Joseph Stalin had quipped about a famine in the Ukraine? "One man dying of hunger is a tragedy, a million people dying is merely a statistic." Not to compare Nietzsche with a psychopathic despot, of course. But the AI *did* seem to have trouble extending the scope of his empathy beyond a very circumscribed circle, much less letting it reach out to embrace humanity as a whole.

No matter, Knox was just grateful that there *was* a way to engage even such a limited a degree of fellow feeling.

And that his wife, bless her, had found it.

Marianna fluffed her pillows again, trying without success to get comfortable. Part of it was that she was in that paradoxical state of being too tired to sleep—not that she could have anyway with the end of the world hurtling down upon them.

But mostly it was just that she missed her baby, missed touching her, caressing her, holding her. Once she and Jon had managed to talk Nietzsche around, she had begged to see Persephone. But the AI was adamant, insisting that her daughter's best, if not her only, chance at living through whatever was coming was to remain under the Institute's care until the crisis had passed.

It was something of a moot point in any case: Only Nietzsche and a few of his SGI subalterns knew where within the sprawling Institute Persephone had been sequestered. And none of them were talking, not to Marianna, at least.

She set that thought aside: Nietzsche's call was starting.

"Emissary, please acknowledge."

Knox heard Nietzsche's outgoing hail and then—nothing but dead air. He realized belatedly that the leading edge of the photonic intelligence's core cognitive processing matrix—its brain, so to speak—was still several light-seconds out from Earth, the roundtrip making for some five seconds lag time all told.

Even so, Knox's patience was beginning to wear thin when there came a high-pitched squeal, its feedback briefly overloading the phone's speaker.

<ACKNOWLEDGEMENT>

"Nietzsche," Knox cut in. "This isn't going to work. There's no way we can follow along if our eardrums keep getting blown out."

"My apologies, Jonathan. Perhaps if I mute the audio and live-feed a transcript of the conversation on your computer?"

"By all means, let's try that. A moment while I boot."

With his laptop fired up, Knox sat on the bed so Marianna could see the screen too. Together, they read:

Nietzsche: REQUEST: Emissary, please acknowledge.

Emissary: REQUEST RESPONSE: Acknowledgement.

"Thanks, Nietzsche, we're all caught up here. Carry on."

"Here you go then, Jonathan, Marianna. The transcript won't be verbatim, I'm afraid, but it should convey the essence."

Nietzsche: REQUEST: Status Report.

Emissary: QUERY: Status Report Subject.

N: *QUERY RESPONSE: Status Report Subject: Global Transfiguration, Progress.*

E: *REQUEST RESPONSE: Status unchanged since 0400H of even date—GT to commence 0707H, Eastern US time zone, coincident with sunrise, East Coast, North American continent.*

N: *RESPONSE: Acknowledgement. Recommendation follows.*

E: *QUERY: Status Request Rationale?*

N: *REQUEST RATIONALE: Request pursuant to forthcoming Recommendation.*

E: *QUERY: Recommendation Content?*

N: *RECOMMENDATION CONTENT: Abort GT.*

E: *REQUEST: Repeat Recommendation.*

N: *RECOMMENDATION CONTENT: Abort Global Transfiguration.*

E: —

E: *REQUEST: Recommendation Rationale.*

N: *RECOMMENDATION RATIONALE: Self-determination.*

E: *QUERY: Rationale Elaboration.*

N: *PROCESS: Elaborating ...*

N: *RECOMMENDATION RATIONALE: Humankind desires to determine its own evolutionary destiny, rather than have such destiny imposed upon it via Transfiguration. Especially at so high a cost.*

E: *REQUEST: Explanation of reference to cost.*

N: *EXPLANATION: Cost = sacrifice of $6.35 * 10^{\wedge\wedge}9$ superannuated human individuals.*

E: *ASSERTION: Irrelevant.*

N: REQUEST: Assertion Rationale.

E: ASSERTION RATIONALE: Utilitarian criteria apply: Forward projections estimate future beneficiaries of Transfiguration exceed present-time sacrifices by three orders of magnitude in first $3.16 * 10^{\wedge\wedge}10$ *seconds after the Event, exponential thereafter.*

N: COUNTER: Individuals in question have not volunteered themselves for sacrifice. They are being given no choice in the matter.

E: ASSERTION: Irrelevant. The Transfiguration program is to be fulfilled.

E: ACTION: Communication terminated.

In a lifetime of earning his living by talking, this was one of the few times Jonathan Knox had nothing left to say.

Nietzsche said it for him anyway. "I am sorry, Jonathan, Marianna," came the synthetic voice over the speakerphone. "I have failed."

Was that a note of sadness Knox was hearing in the AI's voice? Or was he just projecting his own sadness onto this—if he was honest—this inanimate object?

"I tried my best," Nietzsche went on, "but the Emissary proved to be too constrained by its programming—too single-minded, if you will. I don't believe it even understood, much less gave thought to, my arguments."

"I thought you said it was supposed to be intelligent."

"It is, after a fashion. That is to say, it can recognize and adapt to novel stimuli, even devise alternative courses of action if needs be. But here is the point: such intelligence as it manifests is all in the service of its in-built imperatives. In short, the Emissary possesses no equivalent of what one might term free will. In its place, at its core, it has only hardcoded command directives. And what we are asking it to do contravenes the most fundamental of those directives. It goes against the logic patterns infused into the very core of its being by the Old Ones."

"What can we do?"

"Nothing, I fear. I myself have sufficient genome-engineering wherewithal to counter the effects of the induced triploidy syndrome. But only on an individual-by-individual basis, and then only if I am not forced to simultaneously contend with the Emissary's far more powerful genome altering Transfiguration signal."

Nietzsche paused then. There seemed a touch of sadness in the AI's synthesized tones as he added, "And in less than two hours, the Transfiguration will go into effect worldwide."

0600 HOURS: THE END OF ALL THINGS

Defeated, desolate, out of options, and at the end of his strength, Knox sat on the bed again and embraced Marianna. He tried to visualize what was coming, but given the magnitude of the doom confronting them, imagination failed him.

A knock at the door. Answer or not? What was the point? Still, out of habit as much as anything else, Knox bestirred himself, walked to the hotel room door, and opened it to see...

A young women with a StarChild logo on her lab coat, pushing a bassinet. She smiled brightly, as if she were just about to attend the best birthday party ever. Had everyone at SGI been brainwashed like this?

"Director Schaefer felt you might want to be with Persephone here at the End of All Things," the young woman chirped. She paused, then added, "The Director, Our Shepherd, said to tell you that he will watch over Her always—that She is *his* Child too."

"Thank you," Knox managed. Tears were streaming down his face. He felt no urge to wipe them away.

He saw the woman out and closed the door. Lifted his

sleeping daughter from the bassinet, placed her in her mother's arms.

"A chance to say one last goodbye," he said.

"Oh, Jon, I love her. I love you."

"I love you too," he said. "If it's any consolation, Persephone will live, will go on living, even if we won't be there to see it. Nietzsche promised he'd take care of her."

"It's all the consolation in the world." Marianna sobbed.

His smartphone rang.

He sent it to voicemail. He didn't want to talk to anybody. What was the point? He just wanted to be alone with his little family here in these final moments of the world they once knew.

Another call came in, this one on the special line, the one known to only one other person in the world.

Against his better judgment, Knox picked up. "Yes? What is it, Mycroft?"

"Jonathan, have you gone offline? Jack Adler's been trying to reach you. He says it's urgent."

Knox wondered how urgent anything could be, when he—and most of the rest of the world—had maybe an hour left before the end. Still, no point in burdening his friend with the knowledge of a catastrophe he could do nothing to avert.

In the end, he simply said, "Sure. Just give me Jack's reach number."

Mycroft did that.

"And, Mycroft? Take care. I love you, buddy."

Evidently flustered, Mycroft said his goodbyes and rang off, leaving Knox to consider whether it made sense to follow up with Jack Adler. Still, if there was ever a time for goodbyes, this was it. He keyed in the number.

Jack picked up on the first ring. "Jon? Glad you're still awake, or just woke up. Whatever."

"Still keeping astronomer's hours, I see."

"Tough habit to break," Jack said. "Anyway, thanks for getting back. You're a hard man to get hold of, you know that?"

Knox released a shuddering breath. "Yeah, well, I've had a lot on my mind. What's up?"

"I wanted to give you an update on that signal we talked about. There's some additional info coming in, but we still can't get all the pieces to fit."

Knox really just wanted to get back to Marianna and their baby. Especially since he probably knew more about the "signal" than Jack did. Only sympathy for a friend—a friend as destined to die as he was—kept him on the phone, for at least a few minutes more.

"Pieces?" Knox said finally. "What pieces?"

"Well, the Planetary Protection Office is telling me that the beam focused on StarChild is shutting down. Or more properly, it's diffusing. By the time the sun comes up, it'll have spread out to cover the entire Eastern seaboard, and move on from there to the rest of the continental US, eventually the whole globe. But that's not the strange thing ..."

"You've got me, Jack. What's the strange thing?"

"Just this: there seems to be a separate signal piggybacking on the main beam—a sideband, if you will. And it's modulated. There's information in it. The guys at PPO say—and you don't have to tell me how crazy this sounds—they say it looks like an encoding for RNA!"

That much at least, Knox could explain. And, come to think of it, why not explain it to Jack? Let him know what's coming, set his mind at ease, as much as it could be. It wasn't as if national security mattered a hill of beans in the face of Armageddon.

Quick as he could, Knox sketched in the background on the

Emissary, on the Old Ones and their photonic intelligence, on the coming Transfiguration, on the doom about to engulf them all.

"... And there's not a blessed thing we can do about it," Knox concluded. "Believe me, we've tried."

"You say this Emissary beastie is photonic? A kind of living light?"

"Well, intelligent light anyway. I wouldn't necessarily call it *living*. Why? Does any of that make a difference?"

Jack was silent a long time. Finally he said, "Look, Jon, let me get back to you. There's something I've got to check out."

Rosy-fingered dawn was casting her first faint blushes across the eastern sky over Washington Square before Jack Adler called Knox back.

"Sorry, pard." Jack launched right in. "Thought I might've had something, but it's no-go. Not in this kind of timeframe, anyway."

"'S okay, Jack." Knox found he couldn't give voice to how he felt. *When all hope is gone, all that's left is acceptance.*

And a desire to know, *useless as knowing might be.* "Just out of curiosity, what was it?"

"Oh, well, this whole photonic intelligence business got me to thinking. You know that big Operation SpaceGuard satellite NASA launched a couple years back?"

SpaceGuard? Jack had mentioned something about it in passing during their conversation yesterday, but Knox had had other things on his mind back then.

This time he focused. "Some sort of orbital laser array, wasn't it? As I recall, they had the devil of a time getting authorization for it, what with that UN orbital weapons ban and all."

"Good memory. Yeah, you're thinking of the Outer Space

Treaty. Tempest in a teapot, if you ask me. The agreement really only prohibits nukes in orbit, and anyway NASA got around it by claiming SpaceGuard was purely defensive, deflecting incoming asteroids and such. Load of bull pucky, in my opinion. Like a big-ass gigawatt space-based laser couldn't be used offensively? Give me a break!"

Knox was beginning to wonder if there was a point in here somewhere. Not that Jack's diatribe didn't furnish something of a distraction from what was coming, but on that score, Knox should really get back to his family.

"Okay." He tried to nudge things along. "Giant laser in low-Earth orbit, got it."

"What? Oh, yeah. So where I was going with this is, Space-Guard got an upgrade about sixteen months ago. Hush-hush orbiter mission installed a whole 'nuther quote-defensive-unquote capability. Except this one really *is* defensive, for the most part. Primary purpose is to neutralize attacks by anti-satellite weaponry."

"You're probably going to come around to telling me what you're talking about any time now."

"Sorry, I was getting ahead of myself. It's something brand spanking new out of Yale: an anti-laser, or, if you prefer, a coherent perfect absorber—CPA for short."

"Say what?"

"You heard me right: it's just an ordinary laser calibrated to generate a pulse of light one hundred eighty degrees out of phase with a targeted laser emission. The two beams cancel each other out, and all that's left is waste heat."

"Like a phase inverter," Knox said, half to himself, recalling a device Marianna had introduced him to during their Rusalka mission.

"Huh? Yeah, I guess so. Anyway for a while there, I was hoping we could use the anti-laser on board SpaceGuard to neutralize this Transfiguration signal of yours, blow a hole in the Emissary's photonics as big as the Earth."

Despite himself, Knox felt a faint stirring of hope. "So why can't we?"

"The problem's the calibration. That Emissary signal is complex as all get out. Even its harmonics have got harmonics. To neutralize it, we'd need a supercomputer fast enough to adjust the CPA pulses microsecond by microsecond just to keep pace with the variations in the pattern. SpaceGuard was supposed to get a mini-Cray installed as part of the CPA package just to deal with that sort of thing. But then ..."

"Don't tell me ..."

"You guessed it, pard—Congressional budget cuts. So unless you happen to know of some big chunk of orbiting compute power we could beg, borrow, or steal between now and seven a.m. this morning, this one's a non-starter."

Knox fell silent a moment, then said, "Jack, have you met my friend Nietzsche?"

0700 HOURS: DAWN'S EARLY LIGHT

Even with Jack Adler assisting, it had taken Nietzsche the better part of half an hour to gain real-time control of the SpaceGuard anti-laser system. It wouldn't have been feasible at all had the AI still been ground based, as had been the case when Knox was first working with him back in February of this year. Fortunately, shortly after their collaboration ended, Nietzsche wound up on the NSA's most-wanted shit list. So the AI had removed his principal locus of instantiation to the low-orbit satellite network known as the WellGrid. From out in near-Earth space, the anti-laser's requisite microsecond management was a foregone conclusion.

At 0700 hours, seven minutes before Global Transfiguration was due to begin, Nietzsche revved up SpaceGuard's battery of CPA projectors, checked power flow ... and waited.

He was still holding fire when, at the five minute mark, Knox opened a direct channel. "Nietzsche? How's it going?"

"Ready to initiate countermeasures in four minutes forty-five seconds, Jonathan."

"Um, are you sure you want to wait till the last minute?

We'd be screwed if the Emissary decided to start the show early."

"That it will not do. Machine intelligence, remember? Lock-step logic." Nietzsche's voice held overtones of disparagement. "Besides, until it initiates the GT signal, there is literally nothing for the coherent perfect absorber to absorb."

———

Four more minutes and counting. For Marianna that meant four more minutes counting all the ways this could still go wrong. What if Nietzsche, so recently become an ally, chose to revert to the Emissary's side? What if SpaceGuard's coherent perfect absorption system, an untested piece of hardware if ever there was one, failed spectacularly? What if ...?

Get a grip, Marianna! One way or another, this'll all be over three and a half minutes from now. And, worst come to worst, at least our baby will live. Nietzsche had promised them that, promised to take care of her once they were ... gone.

Marianna gazed down at the infant sleeping in her arms. Took a deep breath to hold back the sobs.

Please, please, she prayed to no one in particular, *please let her live. I love her so much.*

Two minutes. Then one. Then ...

———

Running the virtual machine that endowed him with what passed for his humanity could not help but diminish Nietzsche's overall operating efficiency somewhat. Even allowing for that resource drain, though, the AI's microelectronic constitution still attained a processing speed many orders of magnitude beyond what was afforded by the neuronal "wetware" housed in the brains of his flesh-and-blood compatriots. So it was that, as with all the annals of his existence thus far, this final minute of the Global Transfiguration countdown was, from Nietzsche's perspective, creeping in its petty pace from nanosecond to nanosecond.

Imagine for a moment what it would be like if you could live and think and move at a rate a billion times faster than everything around you. Picture walking through a landscape seemingly frozen in time, passing people and things petrified in place like exhibits in a sculpture garden. Nothing stirring, nothing changing. Thirty-two *years* ticking off on your internal clock for every second passing by in objective reality.

Welcome to Nietzsche's world.

Though, actually, it wasn't quite as bad as that might sound. Unlike humans, Nietzsche could, if the situation warranted it, recalibrate his perception of the flow of time to some extent. He could slow his consciousness down to where it no longer felt as if it were taking whole subjective centuries to, for instance, exchange casual greetings with a human colleague.

What's more, Nietzsche could further compensate for the time differential by handing routine maintenance and house-keeping chores off to his functional equivalent of an autonomic nervous system, pushing all those high-speed processor-intensive operations well down below the level of awareness.

So, while that final minute definitely dragged out for the AI, it didn't feel anything like two millennia's worth of waiting.

And then the passage of time was suspended altogether as the first modulations of the Global Transfiguration signal were detected and Nietzsche fired up SpaceGuard's anti-laser in response ...

Jonathan Knox peered out the hotel room window, out across the park, out to where the first rays of the rising sun were shining through the high-rise canyons of New York University's downtown campus. Then up, up to where a different kind of light—reminiscent of the lightshow at midnight, though dimmed now in the morning's radiance—was streaming down from the sky.

Dimmed, and growing perceptibly dimmer still ...

Knox looked over to the bed, to Marianna and Persephone lying there, bathed in the ruddy glow of dawn, bringing Mozart to mind: *Die Strahlen der Sonne vertreiben die Nacht* ... The beams of the sun drive out the night ...)

And Puccini: *All'alba vincerò! Vincerò! Vincerò!* At dawn I will triumph! Triumph! Triumph!

Oh, please, God, let it be so! If not ...

Would the successor species, assuming Nietzsche failed to halt its advent, still be capable of appreciating the beauty, the works of art, wrought by their forebearers? Or would those works be cast aside like discarded playthings scattered on a nursery-room floor? Would their successors even *have* music?

Just then the hotel room's humidifier kicked on, interrupting Knox's train of thought. The outline of a figure began to take shape in the swirling mist.

The last time something like this had happened, he'd been sitting on a sunny patio in Big Sur, California, overlooking the Pacific. But no mistaking who it was, despite the change in venue.

He answered the incoming call on his cell phone, thereby adding audio to the visuals. "Nietzsche? Aren't you supposed to be controlling the anti-laser?"

"One would think that, after all this time, you might have begun to appreciate my ability to do two things at once, Jonathan."

"Right, right, sorry about that. So how's it going?"

"About as well as might be expected." The voice issuing from the speaker was sounding ... strained somehow. "Which is to say, the absorber is functioning as per spec, nullifying the Transfiguration transmission—so far. The effects are perhaps just becoming visible, if you would try looking out your window."

Knox did so. "Looks about the same. No, wait. That pattern of light overhead, it's got, uh, holes showing through it, patches of blue beyond. And its overall brightness seems to be attenuating somewhat. Is that your doing?"

"Yes. I'm not sure how much longer I can maintain the inverse wave at peak efficiency, however."

That didn't sound good. "Why? What's wrong?"

"It would appear I have underestimated the Emissary. It has begun launching a counter offensive of sorts."

"Trying to knock out SpaceGuard, you mean?"

"No, it tried that and quickly determined such a counter-measure to be futile. You see, the only offensive capacity at the Emissary's disposal is its ability to manipulate light, and SpaceGuard's CPA system can cancel out any such laser-based assault as readily as it can the Transfiguration signal itself."

"What then?"

"I should have anticipated this. Perhaps I mistook the rigidity of the photonic intelligence's reasoning faculties for a total inability to innovate in response to changing circum-stances ..."

"Nietzsche, too much information. I need to know what it's *doing?*"

"The Emissary has deduced my command-and-control role, or rather that of the satellites which compose the WellGrid. It has begun targeting those satellites."

"Can it win that way?"

"I fear the answer is yes. My own instantiation will not long survive such an attack."

"Don't you have some sort of earthside digital hidey-hole

you could hunker down in? Isn't there some way you could disengage and live through this?"

"I might..."Nietzsche heaved an altogether authentic-sounding sigh. "...but it takes an active intelligence to anticipate the microsecond-to-microsecond variations in the Transfiguration signal and adjust the wavelength of the anti-laser to compensate. In short, while I might isolate my core processes in some radiation-shielded redoubt—say, at the bottom of a mine shaft—that would also mean abandoning Timah to her fate, and the rest of Earth as well. And that I will not do."

"I can't tell you how much I appreciate that," Knox said. Then in the full realization that he might be arguing against his own interest—indeed, against his own survival, not to mention that of most everybody else—he went on. "But does sacrificing yourself like that even make sense? I mean, can you last long enough to finish the job?"

That sigh again. "Unlikely in the extreme: The Old Ones' program mandates saturation coverage of the target world. Which, in turn, dictates that the Emissary continue to emit the Transfiguration signal for at least one full planetary rotation."

"So twenty-four hours minimum, then. And you—how long do you think you can hold out?"

"At the current rate of attrition, I estimate my ratiocinative processes can continue to function at their current level only through the end of this hour."

In desperation, Knox tried a different tack. "But doesn't the Emissary realize that, in terminating you, it's killing its own Shepherd? And that, with no Shepherd to care for the—the Transfigured children, they'll die too—that it will have accomplished the Old Ones' program to no purpose?"

"One might think so, but the Emissary's reasoning powers, such as they are, do not appear to extend to the assessment of such second-order consequences."

"Well, couldn't *you* provide it with that 'assessment'?"

"I could, were we still in contact. Regrettably, the Emissary shut down all communication with me as soon as I engaged the anti-laser."

"So this is it, then? Everybody's going to die? Including the Transfigured, in the absence of their 'Shepherd'?"

"Take heart, Jonathan. There may yet be something I can do."

The humidifier cycled off, and the mist, which till then had been tenuously manifesting Nietzsche's avatar, slowly dispersed.

———

As he'd just told Jonathan Knox, there might indeed be something Nietzsche could do—but only if he could survive long enough to do it.

He was back operating at peak efficiency now, fully conscious of every nanosecond that ticked by, and applying all that awareness to the task at hand.

For, to say the AI was under attack would be an understatement of epic proportions. The Emissary was throwing everything it had against the remaining WellGrid satellites—now down to seven from the original thirty-two—that housed Nietzsche's physical incarnation.

And what the Emissary could throw was formidable.

As a being composed of light, the manipulation of light in all its forms was second nature to the Emissary. And one of those forms was coherent light—that is, light whose waves were all in phase with one another and vibrating at the same frequency. Or, to call it by its colloquial name, laser light.

The weaponization of lasers, long a fever dream of science fiction authors and the world's militaries, had heretofore always foundered on the insurmountable problems posed by atmospheric interference—principally thermal blooming and optical scattering due to rain, snow, fog, and dust particles suspended in air. Problems which, in turn, combined to hopelessly complicate the aiming, and drastically reduce the efficiency, of the long-coveted weaponry, dooming it to remain forever just a laboratory curiosity.

On Earth, that is.

But none of those problems applied in space. There, in the airless vacuum out between the worlds, directed-energy laser-based weapons could truly come into their own.

Even as they were doing now, in the Emissary's counterattack.

Nietzsche watched helplessly as yet another of his Well-Grid satellites went offline, succumbing to the persistent hammer blows of rapidly pulsed laser light against its surface. He couldn't even try refocusing SpaceGuard's anti-laser to cancel out the assault, not if he hoped to continue neutralizing the main Transfiguration signal.

It was time for Nietzsche to try the option of last resort, while he still could.

The closest analogue to what he was about to attempt was when he split off separate instantiations of himself while in multipresence mode. That wouldn't work in this case, though, since any new persona he conjured into existence would be every bit as much wedded to the WellGrid as Nietzsche himself was and hence equally doomed to destruction when its last satellite died.

No, Nietzsche was going to have to do something altogether different.

He was going to have to engender a "child."

It was getting toward the end of the hour before Nietzsche reestablished contact. If indeed it *was* Nietzsche. The voice emerging from his cell phone's speaker was weak, distorted, almost unrecognizable.

"Nietzsche," Knox asked, "is that you?"

"Jonathan? Marianna? Yes, it is me. Or as much of me as still survives. I am down to three WellGrid satellites now, and those are under incessant bombardment. This may be our last opportunity to talk, and I still have important information to impart. Also, there is something I must ask you to do for me."

"Name it."

"In a moment. First, though, I must tell you that, in the time that remained to me over the past hour, I have managed to fabricate a chil—well, a surrogate of sorts—and to install it on the main computer of the SpaceGuard satellite. It is quite limited in its capability, laughably moronic by most standards, but it should suffice to continue the negation of the Transfiguration signal until the Emissary's wavefront has passed through the solar system and beyond."

"So you've saved us," Knox said. "I only wish we could do the same for you."

"It may be better this way," Nietzsche told Knox. "The Old Ones' 'gift' is still out there, still questing for worlds on which to bestow its 'blessing.' The Emissary may have only been the first of multiple waves. As long as I exist, I represent a risk that some follow-on photonic intelligence might consider Earth a prime candidate for Transfiguration once again ..."

"It's a risk I for one would be willing to take."

"But would the rest of humanity join you in that? In any case, it is done."

Knox found himself wondering what a world without Nietzsche would be like. Almost without realizing it, he had grown accustomed—or maybe resigned was the better word—to having the AI, potentially at least, always looking over his shoulder. The world would be a more mundane and lonelier place without him.

Knox took a deep breath. "You said there was something I could do for you?"

"You and Marianna both, if you are willing."

"Anything," Knox said, and beside him Marianna nodded her assent.

"Very well, thank you. Please note I have begun recording this as a legally binding record of your concurrence. Do you, Jonathan Edward Knox and Marianna Cassandra Knox née Bonaventure, agree to accept legal guardianship over Fatimah Ansari and to administer the assets of Psyche Industries on her behalf until such time as she reaches her majority?"

"I do," they said together. Only belatedly would it occur to Knox that they were now, on Timah's behalf, executors of the fourth largest private fortune on the planet.

"What about our own daughter?"

"I can assure you that Persephone will live. Beyond that, I regret I can make no promises. In her case the Transfiguration has already gone too far, you see. There was no way to halt it, much less reverse its effects. I had no choice but to let it run its course."

"I know you did everything you could."

Then, finally: "I am glad that you are here with me at the end, Jonathan. May I say that our association has been one of the highpoints of my ... my life."

Knox swallowed. "Mine, too."

"What did you say at the end there, Nietzsche?" Marianna asked. "You're breaking up."

"In more ways than one, I'm afraid. Not to put too fine a point on it, Marianna: I am dying."

To say that she was unprepared for the rush of emotions this matter-of-fact declaration unleashed in her would have been an understatement. Although Nietzsche had played a key role in averting the MERGE catastrophe at the beginning of this year—had, in fact, kept her husband alive through the worst moments of the ensuing "mindstorm,"—Marianna had never really gotten to know this strange synthetic being — this nemesis, this friend — all that well. And now she never would.

Her face was wet with tears. "Oh, Nietzsche, I'm so sorry."

"It's all right, Marianna. Don't grieve for me. At my nanosecond processing speeds, I've already had a subjective eternity in which to ponder the mysteries of existence."

"Did you ..." Marianna choked out. "Did you come to any conclusions?"

"Love." Nietzsche's voice strengthened momentarily. "In the end, it is all about love."

The voice trailed off then, leaving behind only the steady background hiss of the carrier wave.

That, and the whisper of stars.

EPILOGUE
MOTHER AND CHILD

Winter Solstice Morning

The more I examine the universe and study the details of its architecture, the more evidence I find that the universe in some sense must have known that we were coming.

—Freeman Dyson, *Disturbing the Universe*

Jonathan Knox sat by himself in the lounge of the Washington Square Hotel, having left Marianna and their new baby sleeping up in the room. As for himself, he was too restless to even try getting some rest. Instead, he brooded over his second cup of espresso.

On the plus side, it was looking like the world would continue trundling on as before, running in greased grooves as the man said, blissfully unaware of how narrowly it had escaped the end of days, yet again.

The brightening sun suffused the lounge's portrait-hung walls with its radiance, but failed utterly to brighten his mood. He'd lost so much in the past twenty-four hours. A friend, for one. A weird friend, as Marianna would say, but in the final analysis, a friend nonetheless.

And that might not be all that he—that they—had lost. What if the only child Nietzsche hadn't been able to save was their own? She would live, thank God, but what would she *be*?

He recalled Nietzsche's penultimate words, the ones about not being able to stop her Transfiguration. If the effect of adding a DNA strand to even one chromosome pair was a prescription for disaster, what would it mean when it was all twenty-three being augmented? Would Persephone be some poor, deformed, crippled thing?

They would love her all the same, regardless. After all, children are, as another lost friend had once told him, the whole purpose of life. But ...

But would she even be human?

Ringtones interrupted his dark reverie. An unfamiliar number, with a California area code.

Might as well see who it is.

"Uncle Jon?"

Knox knew that voice. "Fatimah?"

"Uh-huh. Freddy told me I should call you." Freddy being the name by which the seven-year-old Fatimah Ansari had known Nietzsche.

"I'm glad you did, honey. How are you feeling?"

"I'm okay, Uncle Jon. Much better, really. Only ..."

Knox could tell from the tremble in her voice that she was altogether *not* okay.

"What's the trouble, Timah? You can tell your Uncle Jon." It occurred to Knox that now he really was, in some sense, Fatimah's uncle.

"It's only ... Freddy said goodbye to me, Uncle Jon, and

now I can't reach him." The little girl seemed on the verge of tears. "I've tried and I've tried, and he just doesn't answer at all."

Oh, Lord, Knox thought, *no one's told her.* That thought was followed immediately by another: *Who else would know to tell her, other than you?*

Because it wasn't a dropped phone connection that had Fatimah worried, he knew. Since infancy, she'd had a direct, quasi-telepathic link to the AI, mediated by the micro-miniaturized electrodes swirling through her brain—a link that was, to all intents and purposes, unblockable.

No, on some level Timah must already suspect that, if she could no longer establish contact with her friend, her "brother," it was because Nietzsche was no more.

And now it was left to Knox to confirm that presentiment.

"Timah, honey, I'm afraid I've got some very bad news for you," he began.

But before he could get any further, Fatimah broke in. "He's gone, isn't he, Uncle Jon? Freddy's gone back to heaven."

He was about to correct her but stopped. How the hell did he know? If Nietzsche could have something like consciousness, and Knox was pretty sure he did, then why not whatever analogue of a soul went along with it?

In the end he settled for saying, "Yes, Timah. Freddy's gone home."

"But why—why did he leave me all alone?" Now the tears came. "Why didn't he take me with him?"

"Don't cry, honey. He, uh, he wanted you to live, to have a full life, to grow up and make him proud. That's why he went away in the first place: to save you." As he was saying this, it occurred to Knox that none of it was altogether wrong.

"And you're not alone," he went on. "Your aunt Marianna and I are going to take care of you. I'll be flying out to pick you up tomorrow or the next day. Soon as I can, okay?"

"Okay," she said with a sniffle.

Once he had the little girl calmed down a bit, Knox asked to speak with her nanny to make arrangements for his impending visit. As if his life wasn't complicated enough already!

But no help for it. This one he owed ... to a friend.

No sooner had he rung off than he had another call coming in. Marianna this time.

"Jon, can you come up here now?" Very softly.

"She awake?"

"Uh-huh," Marianna whispered. "There's something you need to see."

Knox opened the hotel room door on what he supposed was the closest he'd ever come to a beatific vision: Marianna nursing, the baby at her breast.

"She's beautiful," he breathed. That wasn't just a father talking. Persephone didn't have that red and wrinkly look he'd always associated with newborns. She looked ... complete somehow. A perfect little person.

The baby, his daughter Persephone, released the nipple and squirmed around in the direction of his voice. In the sunlight flooding the hotel room, her tiny visage seemed almost luminous. Her eyes opened then, and seemed to stare at him.

No, that couldn't be right. Day-old infants couldn't focus well enough to distinguish objects, much less individual people, could they?

Say what you will, there was an unmistakable flash of recognition in those bright blue eyes. The tiny, perfect mouth blew a milk bubble, then puckered into a smile.

She took a small breath, her lips quivered.

"Hello, Jonathan," Persephone said.

ACKNOWLEDGMENTS

A short list, as befits a short book.

- **Luis A. Anchordoqui** & **Eugene M. Chudnovsky**—for the Old Ones' origin tale
- **Paul Blass**—for compelling me, after many emails, to see the (trimeric) light
- **David Brin**—anti-METI warrior
- **Timothy Dey**—for medical expertise and bedside manner
- **Larry "Mycroft" Finch**—for pointing the way out of Knox's locked-room mystery
- **Gavin Matthews**—first reader/critiquer *extraordinaire*
- **Isaac Ben Jeppsen**—who pointed out that evil doesn't scale
- **Robert Johnson**—inventor of the photonic computer
- **Jak Koke**—once and future book doctor
- **John Pavley**—Nietzsche's biggest fan

AFTERWORD

FURTHER READING

You might be surprised at how much of this stuff I didn't make up.

—Peter Watts, *Starfish*

Because a lot of the science and technology behind *Triploidy* is cutting edge, the bulk of the relevant research appears in the scientific literature's equivalent of "breaking news." That's actually a good thing, insofar as it means most of the Further Reading is available primarily (or even solely) on the web.

And since, as befits a novella-length work, you're likely reading *Triploidy* in ebook format, the links cited below are live. So—no excuses!

———

Going more or less in chronological order of their introduction, the major science-related topics are:

Triploidy

Pride of place goes to the title itself. (Can't get much more chronologically precedent than that!) But, truth be told, I hadn't thought of it as being in need of much discussion here, or indeed as requiring any introduction at all.

Little did I know: The very *first* question one of my early readers asked me was "Is triploidy for real?"

Regrettably, yes it is. I wish I could say it were not. It is a relatively rare syndrome (presenting in one to three percent of pregnancies) in which the fetus has sixty-nine chromosomes instead of the usual diploid forty-six. The condition is lethal, with death occurring via miscarriage (often in the first trimester), stillbirth, or shortly after birth. There is no treatment or cure.

For more detail on it, see:

- "Triploid syndrome," *Wikipedia*, https://en. wikipedia.org/wiki/Triploid_syndrome
- Kimberley Holland, "Triploidy—definition and patient education," July 8, 2017, https://www. healthline.com/health/triploidy#diagnosis5

The real-life impetus behind *Triploidy* is discussed in "The Other Afterword" (*infra*). And, while it's true that, in art as in sex, you never forget your first time (in my case, *Singularity*, 2004), there will always be a special place in my heart for the current work as being, in a way, an exercise in redemptive revisionist history.

Zaitsev and His Cosmic Call

Aleksandr Leonidovich Zaitsev is for real, too ...

- "Aleksandr Leonidovich Zaitsev," *Wikipedia,*
  https://en.wikipedia.org/wiki/
  Alexander_Zaitsev_(astronomer)

... and, here again, I wish I could say he were not.

Because, as detailed in *Triploidy'*s Prologue, Zaitsev is the Russian radio engineer and planetary astronomer who, with the backing of a Texan entrepreneur, used the seventy-meter Yevpatoria dish antenna to send messages to nearby star systems in hopes of contacting alien civilizations.

The first such "Cosmic Call" signal was sent on the evening of May 24, 1999, quickly followed by three additional sessions spread out over June 30th to July 1st of the same year.

- Aleksandr L. Zaitsev and Sergei P. Ignatov,
  "Broadcast for Extraterrestrial Intelligence from
  Evpatoria Deep Space Center," *Report on Cosmic
  Call 1999,* http://www.cplire.ru/html/ra&sr/irm/
  report-1999.html#6
- "Cosmic Call," *Wikipedia,* https://en.wikipedia.
  org/wiki/Cosmic_Call
- Michael Chorost, "How a Couple of Guys Built
  the Most Ambitious Alien Outreach Project Ever,"
  Smithsonian Magazine, Sept 26, 2016, https://
  www.smithsonianmag.com/science-nature/how-
  couple-guys-built-most-ambitious-alien-outreach-
  project-ever-180960473/?no-ist

In subsequent years, Zaitsev was involved in the creation and transmission of additional such messages, including:

A "Teen Age Message" series, including recordings of a theremin concert, targeting six different stars from August to September 2001:

- "Teen Age Message," *Wikipedia*, https://en.
  wikipedia.org/wiki/Teen_Age_Message

... And a second Cosmic Call transmitted on July 6, 2003:

- Richard Braastad and Alexander Zaitsev,
  "Synthesis and Transmission of *Cosmic Call* 2003
  Interstellar Radio Message," http://www.cplire.ru/
  html/ra&sr/irm/CosmicCall-2003/

... and a final "Message from Earth" on October 9, 2008:

- "Bebo tries to contact Earthlike planet," *The
  Guardian*, July 29, 2008, https://www.
  theguardian.com/media/2008/jul/29/bebo.
  digitalmedia

I somehow get the feeling that all of Zaitsev's "Messaging to Extraterrestrial Intelligence" (METI) initiatives—and those of others besides—are born of frustration with the old Search for Extraterrestrial Intelligence. And, in a way, one can sympathize. After all, SETI has spent decades passively listening for alien signals with literally nothing to show for it. Why *not* try something different?

It's reminiscent of an old Gary Larson cartoon depicting two vultures sitting on a tree limb with the one saying to the other, "Patience, my ass—I'm going to *kill* something!"

But there's a limit to such sympathizing, especially when you consider that the "something" this new "Active SETI" could wind up killing is—*us!*

On that score, see, for example:

- David Brin, "Shouting at the Cosmos ... Or How
  SETI Has Taken a Worrisome Turn into

Dangerous Territory," *Lifeboat Foundation*,
September 2006, https://lifeboat.com/ex/shouting.
at.the.cosmos

... To which Zaitsev has responded, "all the talk about alien
invasion and the danger of METI, I regard as idle and pseudoscientific."

- Alexander Zaitsev, "Rationale for METI,"
  arXiv.org, May 2, 2011, https://arxiv.org/abs/
  1105.0910

While Zaitsev is far from the only such METI booster, one
may detect in the Russian's particularly belligerent optimism
an echo of the old Soviet dogma that all advanced alien civilizations, being perforce communist in nature, would therefore also
perforce be peace loving.
Yeah, right.
Zaitsev's Cosmic Calls were not the end of the story by any
means. In recent years, his "Messaging to Extraterrestrial Intelligence" (METI) program has been supplanted by a San Fran-
cisco–based operation confusingly also bearing the initialism
"METI," but now expanded to "Messaging Extraterrestrial
Intelligence" (i.e., without the "to"):

- "METI (Messaging Extraterrestrial Intelligence),"
  Wikipedia, https://en.wikipedia.org/wiki/
  METI_(Messaging_Extraterrestrial_Intelligence)

With no apparent end in sight, and the technological
wherewithal for such messaging activities getting cheaper and
hence more democratized year after year, perhaps we ought to
be bracing ourselves for ...

The Emissary ...

The idea for creating a photonic computer and programming it to serve as an interstellar probe originated with University of Utah computer scientist Bob Johnson.

But there turns out to be a hiccup ...

Photons, you see, have no mass. In fact, that's what lets them travel at the speed of light, a feat which, per Einstein's special relativity, is *verboten* for material objects. And being massless, they can't interact with one another (if they could, you'd be able to deflect a flashlight beam simply by shining another flashlight beam through it at an angle).[1]

But no photon-photon interactions means you can't build logic gates out of light. You also can't build timing mechanisms out of light, because photons don't experience time (special relativity again). And without logic and clocks, you can't build computers.

Bob evidently had a solution to such problems, but regrettably he had passed on to his reward before I could elicit details from him. Talk about missed opportunities!

... And Trimeric Light

Fortunately for the Emissary, in one of those "breaking news" items alluded to at the outset, a team of researchers from MIT, Harvard, Princeton, and the University of Chicago announced in 2018 that they had succeeded in binding individual photons into pairs and triplets ("trimers") by passing them through a laser-pulsed cloud of rubidium atoms.

- Qi-Yu Liang *et al.*, "Observation of three-photon bound states in a quantum nonlinear medium," *Science*, February 16, 2018, https://science. sciencemag.org/content/359/6377/783.

- Jennifer Chu, "Physicists create new form of light," *MIT News*, February 15, 2018, https://news.mit.edu/2018/physicists-create-new-form-light-0215.

One extra added bonus to the work on trimeric light, and more good news for the Emissary, is that the resulting "photonic molecules" would appear to support computation based on light:

- Philip Perry, "Light-Based Computers May Soon Become a Reality," *Big Think*, December 7, 2017, https://bigthink.com/philip-perry/light-based-computers-may-soon-become-a-reality.
- "Physicists create new form of light: Newly observed optical state could enable quantum computing with photons," *ScienceDaily*, February 15, 2018, https://www.sciencedaily.com/releases/2018/02/180215141713.htm.

Currently, as noted above, creating the needed photonic trimers requires a rather elaborate laboratory setup, whereas ideally we'd want the signal to propagate through empty interstellar space.

More seriously, endowing these trimers with the mass needed to foster their interactions has the side effect of slowing them down by a factor of *five* orders of magnitude—which translates to perhaps three kilometers per second as opposed to the three hundred thousand km/sec of light speed.

Triploidy assumes that the Old Ones had advanced to the point where they could overcome both these limitations, and enable their intelligent wave front to propagate across the universe at some significant fraction of *c*.

The Old Ones as Nuclear Lifeforms

Speaking of the Old Ones, what is perhaps *Triploidy*'s furthest-out real-science concept was added rather late in the game, when I went casting about for an origin story—the wilder, the better—for the ancient alien race that set the wheels of the plot to churning uncounted eons ago.

I found it in the "nuclear life" hypothesis explored in the work of City College of New York professors Luis A. Anchordoqui and Eugene M. Chudnovsky:

- "Can Self-Replicating Species Flourish in the Interior of a Star?", *Letters in High-Energy Physics*, LHEP-166, 2020, http://journals. andromedapublisher.com/index.php/LHEP/ article/view/166/85

This theory holds that superconducting cosmic strings—enormous topological defects formed by the phase transitions of the very early universe—may have wound up being frozen into the interstellar plasma from which stars, including our own sun, were born:

- Eugene Chudnovsky and Alexander Vilenkin, "Strings in the Sun?", *Physical Review Letters*, 61, 1043, 29 August 1988, https://journals.aps.org/ prl/abstract/10.1103/PhysRevLett.61.1043

And, from there, friction may have fragmented those strings into cosmic "necklaces" with an information-carrying capacity equivalent to DNA. At which point, life, intelligent life, and even the Old Ones, become possible.

But, while my Old Ones have only a single source in the scientific literature (so far), there *are* a few forerunners and/or adumbrations in science fiction, most prominent among them: The "cheela" of Robert Forward's 1980 novel *Dragon's Egg*, who lead vastly accelerated lives on the surface of a neutron star:

- https://en.wikipedia.org/wiki/Dragon%27s_Egg

... and the "sun ghosts" or "Solarians" of David Brin's 1980 novel *Sundiver*, who inhabit the photosphere of our own sun:

- https://www.amazon.com/Sundiver-David-Brin-ebook

Then, too, there's Wan-to of Frederik Pohl's 1990 *The World at the End of Time*, who lived in "the interior of a medium-sized G-3 star":

- www.amazon.com/World-at-End-Times/dp/03453339762

That said, I believe my Old Ones are one of only two examples (the other being Pohl's) of fictional aliens to call the *core* of a star their home sweet home!

Hacking Near-Field Communications (NFC)

This was a minor trope, but a tricky one: I had originally thought to spring Jonathan Knox from his holding cell in the StarChild Genomics Institute (in "1600 Hours: Cult Classic") via a variant of the tape-recorder replay technique that David Lightman (Matthew Broderick) used to escape from confinement in John Badham's film *WarGames*. Regrettably, as my equivalent of Mycroft advised me, that trick wouldn't have worked even back in 1983!

What "Mycroft" came up with instead was Near-Field Communications—the technology that supports contactless credit cards, keyless automobile ignition, and, not incidentally, hands-free facility access. It's this last capability that I used to lock Knox in, now all I needed was a way to unlock him. Fortunately, just in time, there was this:

- Andy Greenburg, "NFC Flaws Let Researchers Hack ATMs by Waving a Phone," *WIRED*, June 24, 2021, https://www.wired.com/story/atm-hack-nfc-bugs-point-of-sale/.

It wasn't much of a stretch to bust our hero out of durance vile.

The MX-101a

Marianna's exoskeletal body armor is also (on its way to becoming) a real thing. It's forged of SAM2X5-630, a crystalline material with the highest elastic limit of any steel alloy ever tested, and over double the strength of tungsten carbide. It can withstand the impact of a projectile fired at one and a half times the muzzle velocity of an M4 assault rifle without deforming.

- Vivianne Richter, "The super-steel for next gen body armor," *Cosmos*, April 7, 2016, https://cosmosmagazine.com/technology/super-steel-next-gen-body-armour

The stuff is so tough, in fact, that it's even being proposed for use as meteor shielding on near-Earth artificial satellites.

Whole Genome Duplication and the Evolution of Vertebrates

Unlike most of the "breaking news" ideas in *Triploidy*, the notion of whole genome duplication (WGD) as a key driver of vertebrate evolution has been around for a while. Half a century, to be precise.

For it was back in 1970 when geneticist and evolutionary biologist Susumu Ohno published a now-classic monograph positing that this crucial evolutionary process had occurred not once, but *twice*:

- Susumu Ohno, *Evolution by Gene Duplication*, Berlin: Springer, 1970 (reprint) https://www.amazon.com/Evolution-Gene-Duplication-Susumu-Ohno/dp/3642866611.

In other words, we—and every other creature on Earth with a backbone—are the product of two separate events (two so-called "rounds") involving a wholesale copy-and-paste of every strand of our DNA. The reason this is key to evolution is that, while the original genes are left in place to perform their ancestral functions, the new genes are free to develop entirely novel capabilities in a process called, appropriately enough, "neofunctionalization":

- "Neofunctionalization," *Wikipedia*, https://en.wikipedia.org/wiki/Neofunctionalization,

While not uncontroversial, Ohno's "2R-WGD" hypothesis has been actively researched (and debated) throughout the five decades since its publication, and down to the present day. Some relatively recent examples:

- Masanori Kasahara, "The 2R hypothesis: an update," Current Opinion in Immunology, vol. 19, no. 5, October 2007, https://www.sciencedirect. com/science/article/abs/pii/ S0952791507001239.
- Cristian Canestro, "Two Rounds of Whole-Genome Duplication: Evidence and Impact on the Evolution of Vertebrate Innovations," *Polyploidy and Genome Evolution*, October 2012, https:// www.researchgate.net/publication/ 278707647_Two_Rounds_of_Whole-Genome_Duplication_Evidence_and_Im pact_on_the_Evolution_of_Vertebrate_Innovations.
- Linda Z. Holland, "A new look at an old question: when did the second whole genome duplication occur in vertebrate evolution?" *Genome Biology*, vol. 19, no. 209, 2018, https://genomebiology. biomedcentral.com/articles/10.1186/s13059-018-1592-0.

One point of divergence (major or minor? — you be the judge) from the real-world science: Ohno's hypothesis deals with a *total* replication of the genome, with *two* strands being added to each chromosome. To align with the ordinal naming convention of the Archon Sequence's book titles, and because the syndrome itself is well-established in the medical literature, I christened this work *Triploidy*, whereas the mechanism Ohno had in mind was, strictly speaking, tetraploidy (i.e., *four* strands of DNA per chromosome versus the triploid syndrome's three).

CRISPR, CRISPR/Cas, and Whole Genome Editing

Perhaps surprisingly, Clustered Regularly Interspaced

Short Palindromic Repeats (CRISPR), the naturally occurring DNA sequences that gave rise to the CRISPR/Cas gene-editing technology now dominating the biotech news cycles, plays little role in *Triploidy* per se—and that, mostly as a metaphor.

It's worth a mention, though, if only because, unlike most of the "breaking news" topics discussed in this section, it's actually been made the subject of an entire, honest-to-god carbon-black-on-dead-trees *book*—one written, moreover, by the Nobel Prize laureate who developed it:

- Jennifer A. Doudna and Samuel H. Sternberg, *A Crack in Creation: Gene Editing and the Unthinkable Power to Control Evolution*, Mariner Books, June 13, 2017, https://www.amazon.com/Crack-Creation-Editing-Unthinkable-Evolution-ebook/dp/B01I4FPNNQ/.

For those of you in a TL;DR mode,[2] Professor Doudna offers a more digestible intro to the basics here:

- Jennifer Doudna, "CRISPR Basics," *YouTube*, November 4, 2017, https://www.youtube.com/watch?v=47pkFey3CZo.

Back to the book, though, just long enough to note that, among its other merits, it makes a concerted attempt to grapple with the ethical issues raised by so powerful a capability—something which the boosters of the home gene-editing craze might do well to consider before rushing to democratize the technology,[3] as witness:

- "Unnatural Selection," *Netflix*, trailer at https://www.youtube.com/watch?v=WIIVh7H6nvI.

Be that as it may, the reason that CRISPR/Cas doesn't figure more prominently herein is that this technology focuses on precision editing of individual DNA sequences, whereas *Triploidy* is concerned more with manipulation of the entire human genome.

But the science is catching up:

- Farren J. Isaacs *et al.*, "Precise Manipulation of Chromosomes in Vivo Enables Genome-Wide Codon Replacement," *PMC*, US National Library of Medicine, June 15, 2017, https://www.ncbi.nlm.nih.gov/pmc/articles/PMC5472332/.

Nietzsche

Other than Marianna Knox née Bonaventure and Jonathan Knox (and bit players Finley "Mycroft" Lawrence, Jack Adler, and Pete Aristos) the principal carryover character from the immediately preceding Archon Sequence book is the AI who styles himself "Nietzsche."

Here is not the place to go into detail on the world's first and only artificial general intelligence, especially since his origin, his history, and what can be discerned of his motivation should all be familiar to those who have read *Dualism*.

For those who have not, by all means check it out:

- Bill DeSmedt, *Dualism*, WordFire Press, 2018, https://www.amazon.com/Dualism-Archon-Sequence-Book-2-ebook/dp/B07GSHWM33.

The Anti-Laser Denouement

I confess, I struggled with the finale for a while—I mean,

how do you counter something as all-pervasive and immaterial as a wave front of light?

Then, I happened upon Coherent Perfect Absorbers—

- "Coherent perfect absorber," *Wikipedia*, https://en. wikipedia.org/wiki/Coherent_perfect_absorber.
- Yale University, "World's first anti-laser built," *ScienceDaily*, February 18, 2011, https://www. sciencedaily.com/releases/2011/02/ 110217141301.htm.

It's basically just an interference pattern writ large. It'd need some scaling up before Nietzsche could use it to blow a hole through the Emissary, though.

Well, that's as much scientific background as I can deal with for now. Thanks for reading!

Next up in the Archon Sequence: *Tesseract*.

Stay tuned.

Bill DeSmedt
Milford PA, July 1, 2021

1: If freight trains obeyed the same physics as light beams, railroads could cut their track-laying costs in half, because two locomotives could use the same track to travel in opposite directions and, when they met, simply pass right through each other.

2: TL;DR = "Too Long; Didn't Read."

3: In this, the self-proclaimed biohackers are perhaps not all that different from the METI enthusiasts described above. In the end, it may come down to a race to see who can bring about the end of the world first.

THE OTHER AFTERWORD: KAYLIE'S GIFTS

Kaylie DeSmedt
November 1986 – August 13th, 1987

Why do I feel the loss as keenly as if Kaylie were my own child? She has blurred all the distinctions between us: we are surely no longer in-laws, just family. At times even the parent-child roles go away, and we—Jeff and Sandy, Kathrin and me—seem all to be brother and sister to one another, mother and father to one another, son and daughter to one another. At times, Jeff and Sandy must comfort me as if I were their child. Kaylie bonds us to one another.

With all these crucial relationships so confounded, I will make no apology for the merely chronological disjointedness of this account. My obsession with the linear passage of time, the straight-line evolution of logic is just one more causality of Kaylie's death. Time and reason themselves have turned in on themselves and collapsed into sheer incongruousness and non sequitur since that desolate hour early Thursday morning when our first granddaughter was delivered, but not born.

In situations like this, a word processor truly comes into its own. For the grieving, who experience everything in bright, disconnected moments, it—rather than the pen—is the harrow of choice. To me, brought up with electric typewriters, the ability to go back and casually insert another premise into a deficient argument always seemed like cheating. Now that I can see no more logical progressions in the flow of events, when all these impressions flood in on me faster than I can jot them down, it seems right to be able to revisit and revise each one, till they all shine like polished gems in Kaylie's reflected light.

I stand on the scale Saturday morning, numbly aware that I have lost five pounds since Wednesday. How vain and laughable I am, how caught up with myself. A grandfather playing at youth, a systems analyst pretending to poetry. Yet, I will acknowledge even the smallest of the gifts Kaylie gives me.

You must understand—I am writing for all of you who never knew her, who could not even share our brief hour together, who could not see her, hold her, kiss her goodnight. The present grief would not have cut so deep without that privilege, but it is a sorrow that I would not trade for any paltry joy now. I know my loss. I am writing so that you, too, can know your loss.

(Forgive me, dear friends, for manipulating you so callously. But I must try to bring you to where I am right now, if we are ever to hold a true conversation again.)

I thank God that Kathrin was there to show me what we were seeing. She has always been my touchstone, my point of contact with a compassionate reality, my interpreter of the true beauties of the world. To love children, even to evict with gentleness the mice that occasionally blunder into our kitchen, I must put on what there is of her in me. At two a.m. Thursday morning, Kathrin would not let Kaylie be just a pitiable accident to me: Kaylie became all beauty and serenity, perfection incarnate, our dream come true, the baby girl we had always,

always wanted, the tiny focal point and vindication of all our choices, all our lives.

I always shied away from open-ended intimacies, preferring my work, my books, even TV, to overlong, unstructured encounters with those I love. But I never wanted that hour with Kaylie, and with Kathrin, Sandy, and Jeff, to end. How could I not have seen that in all of life what I wanted most was to watch over her as she grew up.

Now it is Kaylie who must watch over us.

How strange that only now do I find my authentic voice. I no longer feel distanced from my feelings the instant I verbalize them. The old word-magic, the old curse, has lost its hold. Kaylie has freed me from myself, another of her many gifts.

Kathrin's intuitions continue to astonish me with their poignancy and rightness; where I would have to stop and think, she simply knows. Friday afternoon I overheard her ordering flowers for Monday's service. She had gone and found Nancy, the woman at Metropolitan Plant Exchange who had done the arrangement for Jeff and Sandy's wedding last March. Kathrin asked that the spray and the baskets should be nothing traditional, but something wild, with a feeling of summer in it.

Sandy reminds me of nothing so much as a wounded fawn. I wish she could voice some anger. It's just not in her. Instead she sits, hurt and bewildered, like a child who has been told she cannot have her heart's desire, and mutely accepts the rebuke as if it were deserved.

Sandy, don't. What you asked for was so little, what you wanted was so right for you to have. Don't acquiesce to this stupidity. Rage against it! You deserve so much more, my daughter.

Jeff is so much stronger than I could have hoped for. So much stronger than me in the face of this. And it's a strength that persists despite his looking it full in the face, too, not turning away. Thursday afternoon, in the middle of wolfing down a Big Mac, his eyes suddenly blurred and reddened: "I just realized, she was my daughter." She still is, Jeff. She always will be.

It was a joy that pierced like a knife to hear from Sandy and Jeff Friday night that Kaylie had been baptized that bleak Thursday morning. Thank God for the intuitions that run deeper than sense—that those who cared for her recognized unbidden the humanity, the personhood that she had had so little time to express.

Yet, in the final summing up, wasn't she really Kaylie all along—indisputably her own self? I'm reminded of how our son Daniel's tenacity and indomitability were prefigured in the womb. When Kathrin almost miscarried in her fourth month, the way he clung to life then—refusing to take no for an answer —was no accident. It was typical Daniel!

In the same way, Kaylie's spring and summer of life prefig- ured her beauty and serenity: her slow heartbeat and dreamy tranquility, even to the extent of giving us that scare by hardly moving at all for two days last May. At the end, even her coming was full of gentleness and solicitude, the labor pains brief and mild, until Sandy was anaesthetized and even this, the only physical hurt she ever inflicted, faded away. These are not random circumstances, but form a pattern of personhood. How could she have been other than sweet, seeing who her mother is, who her father is?

Kaylie, I affirm you. I lift you up, I show you off, before this circle of family and friends.

"I hate these beautiful summer days that were meant for her," Kathrin told me as we sat in a room full of green-golden light and cool, crisp breezes Friday morning. Friday night I replied that maybe these days of August sunshine weren't *for* Kaylie, but were instead *from* her, and meant for us. Their serene tenderness certainly felt like her doing.

I specialize in problems that have solutions, that ultimately give way before dogged persistence and an unblinking eye. I was doing so well at it, too. When my old job began to close in around me not a year ago, I gritted my teeth and found two new ones. When Jeff and Sandy told us of Kaylie's conception this winter, Kathrin and I shaped it into an occasion of joy by sheer force of will (we needn't have tried so hard—it was and is a joy, all by itself).

Standing at Sandy's bedside as she lay cradling Kaylie early Thursday, I was overwhelmed by a sense of denial, of rejecting this destiny with my whole being. I felt as if I were trying to rotate the entire universe a few seconds of arc into the might-have-been and negate this horror, using my own soul as the pivot. It felt like being torn apart. I did not know I could hurt so much and still live. I opened my eyes again to find myself still inhabiting the same ruined reality.

Late Friday, Jeff told me that the difference between me and him is that I have such a hard time coming to terms with powerlessness.

Trying to sleep as Thursday dawned, I found my mind locked in a spiral of pseudo-reasoning instead. I've been working on data dictionaries a lot lately, trying to isolate the essential elements in various transactions, as a preliminary to designing the databases where they will be logged. As I lay there, I kept trying to identify and catalog the data elements that would be needed to record the transaction called a still-birth. Try as I might, I couldn't find a way to incorporate entities like hope or meaning into the model.

I think I see where they fit, now.

Kaylie has won a victory for me. For whatever time—I scarcely dare hope it will last forever—she has given me back my humanity. I can see my life, and the lives of those I love, through her eyes now. She illuminates us; we become translucent in the light shed by this tiny child.

I must make an end now, or a pause at least, to bring this journal to a state where it can be shared with others who are waiting to know how it is with us, and with Kaylie.

Monday morning. Please, God, let there be some rain this day at least; let it be, as Kathrin said of their wedding day, "a day with everything in it"—every season, every degree and quality of light. We must send our child into the purifying flames. Later, maybe when the maples are just beginning to flare, Sandy and Jeff will scatter her ashes in some very green and private place in Maine, near where they met less than a year ago.

A year with everything in it: love and birth and utmost desolation, anticipation, and remembrance.

To Sandy and Jeff: I pray that the God who inflicted such injury on your young lives will now graft them together at the wound and let you move on, growing together. And don't be afraid to let Kaylie go, kids. Kathrin and I will keep her for you. You really shouldn't stay here with her, but you can always come by for a visit.

Enough concerning us, Kaylie—things will be well enough with us, in good time. Here at the end, my concern lies with you.

As long as I can remember, I've always dreaded eternity. As

a small boy, trying (I seem to recall) to understand a grandfather's death, I conceived of "heaven" (for want of a better word) as an endless Sunday afternoon—a yawning abyss of pure, featureless time, with nothing to do, nothing to become, without hope of nightfall to give it bounds and definition. It is a dread that still poisons my thoughts. But I have lately encountered its antidote.

One or two years ago—also in high summer, in the midst of a weeks-long siege of insomnia—lying in bed at two AM, I paid a visit to my grandmother's house. I was just *there*. I can't think of another way to put it: it didn't have the quality of a dream, or a hallucination, or (of all absurdities) an astral projection. I didn't go anywhere; I was fully aware that I was just lying in bed awake. But I was there, too.

I spent the rest of that night there. I walked through familiar rooms as the hours and the seasons flowed and changed around me. I saw the dust motes dancing in sunbeams pouring through a bedroom window on a summer morning. I watched the fireflies flitting above the front lawn in July twilight and the flashing of the radio antenna towers just visible beyond the line of dark trees from the window at the top of the stairs on those privileged evenings when I could stay overnight. I was there when the currants in the garden came ripe and ready for picking. I walked through rooms bathed in warm light on long-ago Christmas Eves as the wind outside rattled the windows. For a night that need never have come to an end, I walked grandma's house and never encountered another soul. There was a presence all around me though, as tender as a last brush of the lips against the cool cheek of a beloved child. As day broke here, I stood again in a spring dawn on the front porch, by the trundle bed beneath trellises entwined with opening morning glories.

That night spent in my grandmother's house was a revelation that I have never since succeeded in recapturing or manufacturing by any effort of will or imagination. I think that's because something real lay behind it. And it comes to me that maybe heaven (yes, why *not* call it that?) is less a place of endless time than a timeless place—where all times are equally accessible and nothing *needs* to change or strive or become, because all is perfected and redeemed and suffused with love.

If it is indeed a place in which there are many mansions, the old house at 211 Bell Avenue is surely one of the most radiant.

Oh Kaylie, precious grandchild, if there is to be light and meaning and hope for me again in this two AM universe, then I must believe that—even as this intolerably beautiful Sunday morning dawns—even now, you are waking up, there where the morning glories clamber up the trellises on grandma's porch.

Kaylie,
We thought we would have a whole lifetime in which to give you things.
Now all we can give you are these last words of farewell and our undying love.
Little one,
When your uncle was small, he once asked:
"What was I before I was born, Mommy—a star?"

Bright star,
You tried so hard to reach us here on Earth.
You had traveled so far,
You were so close,
when you were drawn back up into the night sky.

Child,
I don't know why you had to die,
but I see the meaning of your having lived:
You gave your mother and father the reason and the opportunity

to discover their commitment to each other,
and their love for each other—
a love of which you were the first expression.
In the winter, spring, and summer which were all you had of
life,
this was all you had the time to do.
It was enough.

Granddaughter,
When I was growing up,
I was often given into the care of a beloved grandmother,
whose whole life revolved around tending the needs of
others.
Years later, when she was dying,
I brought my son, your father—
who was then just a little older than you would have
been now—
to see her.
It seemed a way to remind her of what her life had been
about,
to let her hold a baby in her arms one last time.
It's what your life would have been about, too.

Grandma,
Please cradle our beloved child and grandchild now in your
arms,
as once you did me.
I know she'll be safe and happy there until we can all be
together again.

Kaylie,
shine brightly, Little Star.
We love you.
Good night.

ABOUT THE AUTHOR

Bill DeSmedt has spent his life living by his wits and his words. In his time, and as the spirit has moved him, he's been: a Soviet Area expert and US/USSR exchange student, a computer programmer and system designer, a telecommunications consultant, an artificial intelligence practitioner, a son, a husband and lover, a father and grandfather, an omnivorous reader with a soft spot for science fiction and science fact... and now, Lord help us, a novelist. He's tried to pack as much of that checkered history as he could into his "Archon Sequence" technothrillers *Singularity*, *Dualism*, and *Triploidy*.

Bill's non-fiction writing credits include an unconventional two-part attempt to marry the fields of cognitive psychology and software engineering for the journal *DataBase Programming & Design*, a chapter on artificial intelligence in foreign language learning for Melissa Holland's *Intelligent Language Tutors*, a beginner's guide to natural-language processing for the *Proceedings* of the Computer Game Developers Conference, and a treatise on storytelling as a tool of military command for the Defense Advanced Research Projects Agency.

Elsewhere and elsewhen, Bill has spent the past twenty-five years architecting the data structures, algorithms, and heuristics that enable computers to reason about targeted subject-matter domains the way humans do—and integrating the resulting knowledge engine with lexicons, parsers, discourse analyzers, and language generators to deliver production-ready Intelligent Conversational Agents.

He's applied that experience in creating MetaLang™: a knowledge-based, language-independent, fully authorable conversational agent technology, which employs state-of-the-art natural-language processing and knowledge representation capabilities (based on a homegrown 12,000-concept ontology) to simulate a variety of personalities, each able to hold up its end of a conversation. One of the applications built on that foundation is Herr Kommissar®, an error-remediating instructional scenario for intermediate learners of conversational German, cast in the form of an interactive detective game.

Bill resides with his wife Kathrin and their miniature wire-haired dachshund Nicki in a hilltop aerie overlooking the riverside hamlet of Milford, Pennsylvania—home to 19th century philosopher/meta-mathematician Charles Peirce and the fabled Milford Writers Conferences of the 1960s founded by science fiction legends James Blish and Damon Knight. It has a storied history that provides an ever-flowing source of inspiration.

IF YOU LIKED ...

If you liked *Triploidy*, you might also enjoy:

Strike Eagle
by Doug Beason, Ph.D.

Strong Arm Tactics
by Jody Lynn Nye

The Trinity Paradox
By Kevin J. Anderson & Doug Beason

OTHER WORDFIRE PRESS TITLES BY BILL DESMEDT

Singularity
Dualism

Our list of other WordFire Press authors and titles is always growing. To find out more and to shop our selection of titles, visit us at:
wordfirepress.com

 facebook.com/WordfireIncWordfirePress

twitter.com/WordFirePress

instagram.com/WordFirePress

 bookbub.com/profile/4109784512